I0534359

Arousal

Susan Hayes

1

CONTENTS

ABOUT THE BOOK   4
DEDICATION   6
PROLOGUE   9
CHAPTER ONE   15
CHAPTER TWO   23
CHAPTER THREE   41
CHAPTER FOUR   59
CHAPTER FIVE   75
CHAPTER SIX   95
CHAPTER SEVEN   113
CHAPTER EIGHT   121
CHAPTER NINE   137
CHAPTER TEN   155
CHAPTER ELEVEN   175
CHAPTER TWELVE   199
ABOUT THE AUTHOR   212

ABOUT THE BOOK

Keri Anderson was looking for a restoration project to distract her from the pain of her divorce and the loss of her grandmother. She found the perfect project at a local antique store: a beautiful, antique bed that called to the artist she'd been before she gave her dreams up to appease a man who hadn't deserved her sacrifice.

Alistair is a prisoner of magic. He's been bound to an ancient bed for nearly two centuries, imprisoned by the spell of a long-vanished sorceress. He's an incubus, a daemon that feeds on sex and pleasure. Roused from his slumber at last, he senses freedom is finally within reach, along with a feast that will restore his powers and slake two hundred years of hunger.

**This book was previously released as *Alistair's Bed*

AROUSAL

SUSAN HAYES

Copyright © 2012 Susan Hayes

Arousal (Book #1 of the Daemons and Angels Series)

Previously sold as Alistair's Bed

First E-book Publication: July 2012

Published by: Black Scroll Publications

DEDICATION

For Mum and Dad, who encouraged me no matter what I was striving for.

And for Karen, for helping me in a thousand different ways.

This book wouldn't exist without all of you

ACKNOWLEDGMENTS

Irene T.

For being the world's most understanding boss

PROLOGUE

Keri was in heaven. She'd always loved antiques; the craftsmanship, the sense of mystery, where they'd been and what they had been part of. Her ex-husband had always preferred modern styles, gleaming and new. Their home had been filled with a never ending parade of shiny new things, each as soulless and empty as their marriage had been.

Now she was free to choose her own style, and somewhere in this dark and wonderful little shop full of treasures, she was certain she'd find the perfect project. Her fingers traced over the carved armrest of a mahogany settee, and she sighed softly at the rich feel of the wood. It hadn't been her intention to spend the day wandering through the dark corners of this little store, but something had prompted her to break with her usual routine and walk up the small alley just a few blocks from her apartment. When she'd spotted the sign advertising antiques and treasures she knew she had to go in.

She shook her head, a chaotic tumble of red waves flying around her shoulders as Keri laughed at herself. Whimsical wasn't her usual approach to life, but today it just felt right. She absently tried to tame her unruly hair as she explored the haphazard stacks of furniture.

She had just gone deeper into the store when Keri thought she heard someone speak just behind her. Startled, she stepped back, tripping over a half hidden footstool and finally landing in an embarrassing tangle of limbs on the floor. Dust flew up in a cloud, and she coughed, feeling utterly foolish.

"You alright back there? I thought I heard a thump." A voice came from the front of the shop.

Oh no, the owner. Please don't let him come back and find me in a heap on his floor.

"I'm fine, just bumped into a chair." She called out and stood, her hand latching onto the first solid thing she could find to help her regain her feet. The moment her hand touched wood, she heard it again, fainter than a voice, but still, she knew she'd heard *something*.

Keri turned to look at what she'd latched onto, and her jaw dropped in amazement. It was a bed. But not just a bed, it was a work of art. The headboard was hand carved, as were the four columns that formed an arching canopy overhead. Every inch of rosewood had been lovingly sculpted, and even beneath the grime piled on by of years of neglect she could detect a patina of aged wood, once well cared for. Without even considering what she was doing, she crawled into the chaos and started excavating her discovery. The more she uncovered of it, the more she loved it. She'd found her first project, she was going to restore this bed.

The store owner had been surprised at her choice, scratching his head as he stared at the massive piece. "That's been there as long as I've had the shop. Came with the place I think. Got no paperwork on it, but if you'd like to have it, Miss, I'll get my boys to haul it out of there for you. Might take a few days, if that's alright?"

"That would be fine, I'm going to need a few days to get the supplies I need to clean it up." She ran a hand down one of the carved columns.

"It seems to be in fairly good shape, it just needs some elbow grease and attention."

"Don't we all Miss, don't we all." He chuckled and inclined his balding head towards the front of the store. "If you'll follow me, we'll get your address and information for delivery and then you can be on your way."

As they wrote up the sale, Keri surprised herself when she gave the address for delivery. Not to her small, overpriced apartment in Vancouver, but to the house she'd grown up in off the coast of British Columbia, a place she hadn't visited more than a handful of times in the past ten years. With her grandmother's passing, it had been left to her, but she'd not yet screwed up the courage to go back for more than a few hours.

As he'd noted down her address, he'd frowned. "Salt Spring Island? That's going to cost you a bit more. I didn't expect to be sending the boys on a ferry ride."

"It's no problem, I expected it," she smiled as she acknowledged the longer drive.

"Nice out there, but a bit remote for me. You're an artist then? There seems to be an awful lot of them living out there."

Keri laughed. "Quite a few, but I'm not one of them. At least, not yet. I like working with wood, though."

* * * *

Alistair's mind stirred, shaking off the darkness for a moment as something brushed past his awareness. He'd been dreaming for what felt like an eternity, adrift in the void so long he wasn't sure if he could feel anything anymore. But there was something, no; there was *someone* out there, her energy felt as light as a gossamer web as brushed over his awareness again. He pushed at the magic that bound him and felt it give a little.

"I am here." He directed the thought towards the unknown woman whose spirit called out to him.

Alistair felt the connection grow stronger, and a sizzling bolt of heat surged through him as somewhere out there, the source of the energy reached out and touched his prison. He gathered what remained of his power and pushed again, harder than he'd dare attempt in decades.

The magic wavered, weakening once more and Alistair put all his effort into slamming one last message through the crack before it could seal him off again. "Help me." He screamed into the darkness until exhaustion forced him to sleep once again. This time, though, he dreamed of a nameless woman. One whose soul called out to him so strongly he could feel her even through the magic that had imprisoned him for more than two centuries.

CHAPTER ONE

Keri stood on the deck of the Skeena Queen ferry, the wind tangling her hair as she watched them approach the harbor and her new home. "What am I doing?" She asked herself, the wind stealing away the words as she glanced back at her little hatchback, crammed to the roof with the material summary of her life. "Not much to show for a lifetime." It had been almost too easy to make the move back to Salt Spring, she hadn't realized just how tenuous her connections to her old life had been. A few phone calls and the rental of a storage locker for her larger furnishings and she was free to leave, just like that. She didn't let herself spend too long thinking about what that meant about the current state of her life. What counted was that she was starting fresh.

Driving out of the harbor she'd been amazed at how many people crowded the area, tourists and summer residents swelling the local population far past its usual number. She made her way to the house, pleased to note that the neighbors had been taking care of the garden, just as they promised. As she drove through the gate, the scent of lavender greeted her, and she knew she was home.

The bungalow was just the same as it always had been, a bit older perhaps, the paint fading a little, the garden not as tidy as her grandmother would have kept it. Keri felt her spirit lift as her feet hit the gravel-lined path to the front door. Inside things were just as she had left them, the furniture shrouded in old sheets, a light layer of dust on everything and a hint of stale must in the air. She threw open the windows and doors and started to unpack.

She had spent the next two days cleaning and organizing things, throwing herself into the manual tasks with enjoyment. She reclaimed every inch of the house from dust and neglect, the scent of pine-sol and wood polish oddly comforting as she worked.

By the time the delivery van had lumbered up the lane to her new home, Keri was ready. The two men were burly, friendly sorts who had clearly enjoyed the leisurely journey to the island and were in good spirits as they had introduced themselves to Keri before beginning to unload her new project.

The bed had been broken down into pieces, and they'd been careful with every part, easing the awkward frame through the bungalow's narrow hallway and down to the master bedroom as Keri watched, eager to get started. "Can I offer either of you a glass of lemonade in thanks?" She'd offered as they settled the last piece into an empty corner.

"Sounds good to me." They'd chimed in, in unison.

She'd poured them both a glass and then joined them in the bedroom, looking at the pieces with her first inkling of concern. "It's like a giant jigsaw puzzle."

"Not to worry Miss, it's relatively easy." The older of the two men had taken another swallow of lemonade and set it aside, moving to where the pieces were settled. "You see this here? Simple tongue and groove set up. This bed was made to last, and they did it without screws or nails." He rested a hand atop one of the columns.

"We've laid it out roughly in the right order; you just need to fit them together again. Nice bit of craftsmanship here, you got yourself an amazing piece."

"Thank you." She felt her worry ease as his explanation allowed her to visualize how the bed would go back together again. It had been beautiful back in the dim shadows of the shop, but here in her bright and cheery bedroom, it was even more amazing than she remembered.

Amazing, And a whole lot bigger. She'd taken measurements before she'd left the shop and known it would take a king sized mattress to fill the massive frame, but even that knowledge hadn't prepared her for how much room it took up, or how much work it was going to take to restore it to its former glory. As she walked the men back to their truck and saw them off, she drove her doubts away. "It's mine, bought with my own money and with no one's input but my own, and I will make this work."

She gathered up her supplies and crouched beside the headboard, it was time to get started. She went over every inch with a soft brush and a gentle cleanser, cleaning away decades of dirt and grime. It was painstaking work, but every time she looked up she could see the progress she had made and it inspired her to keep going. Seated on the hardwood floors of her bedroom with her back aching and the taste of dust in her throat, she let her mind drift as her hands worked.

It had been a hard year. First, there had been the divorce, and then her Gran's death. She'd been trapped in an emotional free fall; struggling to keep herself afloat while everything she had built her life around had been torn away.

Her heart panged as she thought of her dead marriage. She'd tried so hard to be everything Brent wanted, she'd starved herself while cooking him fantastic meals, worn the clothes he liked, kept his house and entertained his friends and co-workers at the parties he'd love to host.

She'd done everything he'd ever asked of her, but in the end, it hadn't been enough, she hadn't been enough. Their lawyers had carved up the life they'd shared and called it a day, and then Brent had carved up her heart by marrying again, only a month after their divorce had been finalized.

She'd heard about it from friends, a destination wedding in Jamaica, a three-month honeymoon in Europe. All the places he'd never wanted to take her, he had taken his new wife instead. She scrubbed harder, the wood gleaming under her fingers. "His new, younger, silicon enhanced wife." She muttered aloud. "Everything you'll never be."

Her eyes burned and stung and she realized she was crying. She hadn't cried in almost a year, wouldn't let herself give in to the temptation. There'd been too much to do to give in to tears and grief. Now, though, she had time.

She let the tears fall, scrubbing them into the wood as she grieved for what she'd lost.

Her tears ended just as she finished cleaning up the last piece, her legs aching as she stood up and stretched, earning another round of protests from abused and forgotten muscles.

"You're too old to be crawling around on hard floors for hours without feeling it." She chided herself as she gazed at her day's work. The wood gleamed in the evening sun, glowing brightly in spots where she'd uncovered swirls of inlaid silver, so dark with tarnish it hadn't been visible until she'd cleaned and polished it.

Standing there, she felt another pang and wished with all her heart that her Gran was there to share this moment. She'd have understood why Keri loved this bed, she'd have loved it too. Keri closed her eyes and whispered a prayer of thanks to her grandmother, for all the years of love and support she'd offered, and for understanding how much she'd needed a place to hide away and heal.

This entire place was a balm to her wounded heart, and she realized now that should have come home months ago.

As she shed her filthy clothes and stepped into the shower, she could almost hear her Gran telling her, *"You're here now, that's all that matters."*

Back in the bedroom, the rays of the setting sun fell on a medallion of beaten silver embedded onto the top of one of the soaring columns. For a moment it flared with a blue-green light that seemed to shimmer and dance as it flowed over the entire frame, leaping from piece to piece before vanishing back into the metal disc.

Somewhere in the void, Alistair's mind stirred again, sensing that change was coming after so many years of emptiness. If daemons had gods, he'd have said a prayer of thanks, but instead, he simply drifted, remembering.

He'd been young when she'd captured him, young and arrogant and foolhardy. Just the sort of incubus that treacherous bitch of a sorceress had been hoping to attract with her sensual summons. He'd ignored every bit of advice and teaching the Elders had given him and gone rushing off to investigate the tantalizing offer he could sense within the spell, never for one minute considering that he wouldn't be able to deal with the wielder of such powerful magic. He was his father's son, powerful and respected despite his youth.

His thoughts shifted colors, a ripple of humorless laughter coursed through him. He'd been a fool.

At first, he'd raged at her, the sorceress who had captured him. He'd raged and fought and threatened to tear her limb from limb if she dared approach him.

For months he'd fought, growing weaker all the time. She'd waited, watching, laughing at him all the while. When he was finally too weak to rage any longer, she'd given him what he needed, sustenance, life.

He'd taken it, hating himself every second as he'd used the woman he'd been offered, feeding off her pleasure until he was drunk with sex and lust, sated and full. The next morning his lover was gone, taken away, and he'd raged again.

Angry and wild he'd done all he could to break free, but he wasn't strong enough to break the spells that bound him to the bed she'd crafted to trap him and keep him forever. He'd never been strong enough.

CHAPTER TWO

The next morning she woke up and groaned, feeling every ache and pain she'd inflicted on herself while working on her project. A week of sleeping on the couch wasn't helping either, but she was determined that the next time she slept in a bed, it would be *her* bed.

Glorying in a shower where water pressure and temperature were not dictated by the number of neighboring apartments drawing on the same plumbing, she lingered under the soothing warmth until the hot water tank was empty. By the time she emerged she was nearly glowing pink with the heat, her aches and pains banished for the time being.

She changed into her work clothes and padded barefoot to the kitchen to pour a cup of coffee from the coffee maker she'd programmed the night before, only then did she let herself go back to the main bedroom to look at her prized possession. She took a step into the room, stopped and did a double-take. "Wow." Was all she could say as she stared at the bed. It didn't seem possible she'd managed to accomplish so much in only a single day.

The wood positively glowed, and every bit of silver shone like a bright river of light flowing through the wood. Bending down she ran a finger over a swirl of inlaid silver, amazed, "whatever is in that cleanser is magical stuff." She drank her coffee as she went over each piece, her deep love for all things wood making her smile as she realized yet again just what an amazing find she'd made in the dusty little shop

Her coffee done, Keri headed back to the kitchen and pulled out a high fiber breakfast bar from the cupboard, nibbling on it as she wandered, still barefoot, out into her front yard to pick up the weekend paper, nearly startled out of her wits by a woman's laughter coming from behind a lilac bush.

"Please tell me that isn't your breakfast."

"Um, yes?" Keri answered the voice, not at all certain who she was speaking too.

"That's not food, that's a gastronomic abomination." A cheerful face framed in silver curls appeared around one side of the lilac, grinning. "Hi, sorry if I startled you. I was just chasing down today's batch of eggs, and I noticed you coming outside. "I'm Samantha Evans, your neighbor, and a dietary busybody."

Samantha appeared to be in her late fifties, smiling as she offered her hand, the other carefully holding closed an apron full of brown eggs.

"Hi there, I'm Keri

Anderson, nice to meet you," she took the offered hand and laughed, feeling foolish in her bare feet and worn out t-shirt. "Sorry, I'm not really dressed for visiting."

"Oh I know who you are, the whole place is abuzz with the news that Tammy's granddaughter has finally come back to the island. And don't you worry about your dress style dear, this is the island, you know that doesn't matter. We moved in just last year, your grandmother was always talking about you."

Samantha winced. "I'm babbling, aren't I? Sorry, I'm just so pleased to meet you. There aren't too many folks up this way and some days I just get a little squirrelly with only my husband to talk to. If I get to be too much of a bother, you just let me know."

"Did you use to visit my grandmother?"

"Every day she'd let me. We'd sit and trade stories about who'd heard from which of their families and wonder what the gossiping gals in town were going to natter on about the next time we set foot in Ganges. You know how it is."

Keri laughed and nodded. "I remember. Are you the one who left the note saying you'd take care of the place for me?"

"That was me. I thought you'd have enough to do without worrying about things here." Samantha reached out and patted Keri's arm. "Tammy was worried about you, after the divorce. She'd be very happy to know you'd come home."

Without warning she changed the subject, reaching into her apron and handing Keri a pair of still warm eggs. "Now, you head on in and make yourself a proper breakfast. You've got an open invitation to come over and visit anytime you like, and if you find any of my girls nesting on your property, just take the eggs as rent."

"Thank you," She gave the older woman a grateful smile, warmth blooming in her chest at the woman's simple but generous gesture. "For everything. I'll come by as soon as I've gotten myself sorted out, I promise."

"You do that dear, and welcome home."

Keri headed back inside, set the eggs down on the counter and started rummaging through the fridge, her breakfast bar forgotten. She was going to make herself a proper island breakfast, hold the guilt; and then she was going to start putting her life in order, starting with her new bed.

After a breakfast of fresh eggs, island cured bacon and thick slabs of buttered toast, Keri eased herself back onto the floor and picked up a rag from the pile she'd brought in for the next stage. "Time to burn off some of that breakfast!"

The hours had flown past as she buffed and polished the entire frame again, her fingers brushing over the intricate carvings with the appreciation only another artist can have for such work. Just touching the carvings made her itch to begin carving again, a feeling she hadn't had in a very long time. Every inch of the wood she was polishing had been worked into complex patterns that were almost hypnotic if she stared at them too long. She'd polished the silver inlay too, admiring the depth it gave the wood. Someone had taken a great deal of effort to make this bed into a masterpiece, and she couldn't believe it was hers.

The one odd thing she'd discovered was the silver medallion embedded into the top of one of the columns. There was only the one, and none of the other columns appeared to have been made to hold one. The lack of symmetry didn't seem right to Keri at all.

"Why just the one?" She wondered aloud. "And why such an ugly thing on such a beautiful bed?" She stared at the disc, wrinkling her nose in distaste at the image it held. A man's form was carved into the metal, his limbs bound with chains and his mouth open in a silent scream.

"Very creepy, but if I remove it I'm likely to find out someday I destroyed a priceless heirloom, so I guess it stays. At least I won't have to look at it once this is all back together."

It took her over an hour to wrestle the various parts back into place, what had seemed simple when it had been explained to her the previous day proved to be a whole lot more challenging when it was just her versus a lot of heavy, awkwardly shaped bits of wood.

It had taken her another half an hour to drag her new king sized mattress out of the hallway and into place, and by the time she was done she was ready to fall onto of her new acquisition and sleep for a week. Breathless and sweating, Keri leaned back against the door frame and grinned. It was perfect.

With the last of her energy, she cleaned up the rags, drop cloths and other supplies, still hardly able to believe that it had taken so little work to bring wood back to its glory.

"I think I've earned a nap." Stripping her clothes off into a pile Keri launched herself into the middle of the bed and fell back, spread-eagled. She burst out laughing when she discovered that the bed was so massive she couldn't touch the edges. "What was I thinking buying the biggest, most sinfully beautiful bed in the world so I can sleep in it alone?"

That single thought reminded Keri of just how lonesome her new life was. There wasn't a soul in the world she could even call to share her excitement over her new bed, or her plans to take up woodworking again. Some of the dazzle left her day, and she curled up under the covers, pulling one of the pillows lengthwise beside her body, wrapping her arm around it and resting her cheek on cool cotton. When a single tear of loneliness trickled down her cheek, she ignored it and willed herself to sleep.

It didn't take long for her to fall into a dream, one that felt terribly familiar. It should, she'd had it countless times in the last few months. She was walking alone on a beach she had never seen in life. The ocean was the color of granite, and the waves crashed high on the sand. She had lost something, something precious, but she didn't know what it was, only that it was gone, and she needed it back.

She started to jog, then to run, her bare feet stinging from the stones and shells she stepped on. The wind came up and tossed sea spray in her face, blinding her. Unable to see she tripped and fell to her knees with a sob.

Part of her cringed, knowing what came next: the sense of failure and then the massive wave that would rise up and crush her. The dream always ended just as the cold water surged over her, blocking out the world.

This time, though, the dream changed. Someone was with her. A pair of strong hands lifted her off the sand, cradling her close to a warm chest. She threw her arms around her rescuer and clung to him tightly as he carried her away from the storm.

* * * *

Deep in the void Alistair had felt her energy, savoring it like the finest of wines. It had been so long since he'd touched the essence of any woman, but this one— he could already sense her passion, her strength. His first meal in centuries would be no paltry mouthful, she would offer him a feast.

As the woman fell deeper into slumber he sent out delicate tendrils of thought, linking her mind to his. He slid into her thoughts and touched her memories, a skill all his brethren shared. Seduction was so much easier when you knew your target's language and customs; what they craved, what they yearned for most. He found her name, *Keri*. He tamped down his hunger and focused, gleaning what he needed to know before gathering what little strength he had left and weaving himself into her dreams.

He'd never experienced another person's nightmare before, nightmares were hardly the easiest place to start a seduction from, but he hadn't got the energy or the patience to wait for an easier dream to step into. His gaze dropped to the red haired woman in his arms as he cradled her closer. It had been hard to watch her fear and pain grow, to wait for the right time to appear. The moment he'd seen her, he'd wanted to save her, protect her from the darkness of her own mind. Such courage and so much sadness blended together in one beautiful package.

He leaned down and brushed a kiss to her brow, feeling his hunger leap at even that small touch. By Styx, he needed this woman, wanted her beyond anything he'd felt before, and they'd only met in a single dream. What would it feel like when he was strong enough to stand in her world and hold her for real? He couldn't wait to find out.

He focused for a moment and let the nightmare fall away, creating a bower of sunlight and blossoms around them, warmth and softness instead of cruel wind and cold sand. Firmly in control of the dream now, he lowered her to the ground and brushed a kiss over her lips, banishing their clothing with a thought.

Beneath him Keri stirred, her fingers stroking over bare skin and her eyes fluttering open to stare up at him in surprise. "You're new," she murmured.

* * * *

Where did I conjure him up from? Keri wondered as she took a moment to appreciate her own imagination. He was gorgeous. Powerful shoulders and a broad chest loomed in her vision, and she could feel the hard muscle and sinew that moved beneath her fingers as she touched him. His face could have been sculpted by one of the great artists, strong lines and bold features set off by a pair of golden brown eyes that seemed to shimmer with heat as he watched her from behind a lock of dark hair that fell over his eyes.

"Aye, I am new, my name is Alistair." She could hear the laughter barely restrained in his voice as he leaned down to kiss her again. "I thought you needed a bit of help back there."

"I did, thank you." She reached up to his cheek to cup it gently. "I like this ending much better." He kissed her a third time, this time holding nothing back as his lips slanted over hers, laying claim to them with a kiss that sent her heart racing.

"I promise this isn't the end, just the beginning." He pulled back just enough for them to catch their breath, his hands gliding over her shoulders and down to cup her naked breasts. "I want to savor you, taste you." He stole another kiss from her lips before letting his mouth wander, blazing fiery trails along her jaw and down towards her captured breasts. "May I Keri, please?"

Her body answered before she could dare speak the words, arching herself up to him in clear invitation even as her fingers tangled in his dark hair, tugging his mouth nearer.

"Say it, Keri, say the words." He urged her, his breath warm as it flowed over her bare skin.

"Please, taste me."

Heat flared in his eyes at her words. "Taste me Alistair." He prompted her.

33

"Alistair please." She whispered her plea, "Taste me, touch me."

His head dropped to her breasts, nibbling and nuzzling them with a low groan. "So sweet." He drew one hardening nipple deep into the heat of his mouth, teasing her with his tongue. "You are making me hungry Keri." He muttered against her skin. With one last flick of his tongue, he released her breast and moved to the other one his movement bringing his rapidly hardening cock up against her hip.

She shifted her body, turning so her soft thigh brushed against his hot, hard length. Her hips moved slowly, their bodies brushing together with a light friction that only made her crave more of him. He groaned, apparently unable to resist her unspoken invitation as his hand left her breast to glide down her body. Flank, hip, thigh, his fingers slowly circling back up to brush against the soft curls at the apex of her thighs. "Yes, please." Keri heard the decadent words and realized she had spoken them aloud.

Her dream lover tore his lips from her breast as his fingers moved to part her folds, stroking her with bold confidence as he found her mouth with his and branded it with a kiss that stole the breath from her lungs. She opened her mouth to his, her tongue darting past his lips to taste the dark cavern of his mouth.

"Alistair," Keri whispered his name against his lips, arching her sex into his questing fingers. He nodded in understanding and slipped his fingers deeper into the slick heat of her folds, pressing into her clit with his fingertips. She moaned and bucked against his hand again, increasing the pressure. Desire bloomed deep within her, a firestorm of the need for his touch, for his lips. His fingers slid deeper still, burying themselves in her channel and she cried out as an orgasm ripped through her without warning. Nothing had ever felt like this, waking or dreaming.

He kissed her again, his mouth drawing in her low moans of pleasure as if he were savoring each and every one. It was though he were feeding on her sighs, drinking her in like a fine wine. While her inner walls still pulsed around his fingers, his thumb sought out the hidden pearl of her clitoris and stroked it firmly, sending another ripple of need through her body.

Keri panted and mewled as he touched her, her fingers skimming across the flat planes of his chest, tracing the hard lines of muscle under his skin. She lowered her lips to his shoulder, drawing in his scent; a subtle mix of spices and musk. His mouth stole downward again, leaving her lips to brand a chain of kisses back to her breasts. He buried his face between them, drawing another soft cry of need from her sweet mouth as his warm breath fanned over her skin.

He moved lower, over the lush curve of her stomach and down until his breath flowed over the fiery red curls that hid her mound. He inhaled her sharply as his fingers moved, withdrawing to expose her every secret to his gaze.

"Beautiful." He whispered and then his mouth was busy, his thumb replaced by the insistent rasp of his tongue over her clit.

Pleasure shot through her, and Keri's fingers tightened, her nail's raking along his shoulders as she felt another orgasm build. He drew her clit into his mouth and groaned, the vibrations only adding to her pleasure. His fingers slid into her tight passage, and she shuddered, arching into him with a soft cry as his fingers found their target. His tongue swirled around her clitoris again and again and then she was lost, falling into a whirlwind of pleasure that stole her breath and left her dizzy and dazed. Her eyes fluttered opened, and she gasped as she stared into his eyes as they flared golden and amber with heat.

"Give yourself to me sweet Keri." His voice was a low growl full of need as he stared down at her, his body covering hers.

"Given, granted, yes." She babbled, laughing as her arms wrapped around his neck and she drew him down and kissed him. "My dream lover, you can have me anytime you like."

Amusement glittered in his eyes as he returned her kiss, his tongue twining with hers as he eased himself into the cradle of her thighs, one hand resting on her knee, coaxing her to wrap her leg around his hips. Thick and heavy he pressed against her, teasing them both as he spread her sex and then withdrew, only to arch his hips into her again. Again and again, he teased her, each time pressing deeper before withdrawing.

Soon she was panting, aching for him to take her completely. As he tried to withdraw again, she flexed her legs and arched her back, impaling herself on his cock until he was buried to the base. With a wild cry of triumph she grinned up at him, her vaginal walls holding him tightly as she locked her legs tighter around his hips.

"No more teasing, I can't take it."

"Aye, no more teasing." He promised and kissed her smiling lips. "Now we let ourselves go." Without any further warning, he began to move, using his powerful physique to lift them both from the bed and then down again, driving himself deeper.

She loosened her thighs, opening space between them, space he reclaimed with every eager thrust of his hips. Around them the dream world blurred into a background of color and light, collapsing into a bubble where only the two of them existed, entwined and racing towards ecstasy.

Every thrust drove Keri further into bliss, her body completely filled by Alistair's impressive cock. She moaned, lifting her head to press a kiss his shoulder, craving the taste of him. Deep in her body she could feel him, hard as marble as he sheathed himself. He groaned again, "I could stay here, inside you forever."

His thrusts grew faster, harder, and Keri watched the expression on his face grow more intense as he reached the limits of control just as she broke and went tumbling into the abyss. She heard herself cry out his name and then her world exploded into sensation and color and she was lost to everything but the pleasure coursing through her. A moment later he thrust into her and shuddered as he came, his roars of satisfaction as he emptied himself into her womb turning to a roar of rage and denial that quickly faded away as the dream came to an end and he was gone.

Keri woke up, stunned. Her heart pounded, and she still felt the echoes of the orgasm she'd just had. "That was one hell of a dream." She muttered dazedly as she sat up and stretched. The sun was still bright outside her window, and she realized that she'd not been asleep more than an hour or so.

She rose and tugged on fresh clothing, still in a bit of a daze. She knew she needed groceries, so she dragged her hair back into a ponytail and headed into town.

All through the drive, her thoughts kept circling back to a haunting image of dark hair and golden eyes, watching her.

CHAPTER THREE

Alistair rested in the void, gathering his newly found strength. Keri had left the small area he could sense, leaving him alone once more. He had felt her energy dancing in his awareness like a firefly in the dark, and now that she was gone he missed her presence. He laughed at himself, the captive daemon waiting in the darkness for a mere human to return. How the mighty had fallen.

There had been a time he had traveled throughout this world and others, nearly drunk with the power he had consumed as he seduced mortal woman after mortal woman. There had been so many, their names and faces had blurred. Everywhere he'd gone there had been willing partners, cloistered daughters and young brides married to old men who could not please them. They'd been so ripe, so full of untapped passions; each one had increased his power and added to his abilities.

And now he lay here, alone and waiting for a single woman to come back to him, so weak he could not even exist in her world long enough to seduce her properly.

He stopped his thoughts and quieted his mind, assessing his strength. Not strong enough to stay in her world, no.

Yet— he willed himself to shift planes, felt the tingle as he passed through the veil and stepped into Keri's room. He drew in a lungful of air and grinned as his senses adjusted to a world of light and scent and sound. *By Styx I've missed this!* He turned and looked at the bed, his eyes glittering with hatred as he ran a hand over a carved column. He'd forgotten what his prison looked like from this side.

He could feel the magic flow beneath his fingers, spells imbued throughout the wood and metal to form a cage he had never been able to escape. Alistair dropped his hand and stepped away from the bed, testing the limits of his prison. Sure enough, five strides from the bed he hit a magical barrier that would not give way. Still, it was better than the void.

He checked his reserves, knowing the small amount of energy he'd gained from his dream encounter with Keri wasn't going to let him stay for long. The dream world was too insubstantial for that sort of feeding. Still, it was a good beginning, his first true seduction in two centuries or so.

He explored her room, amazed at the contents of her closet and dresser. So many colors and half a dozen fabrics he had never seen before. A grin flickered over his lips as he discovered a drawer full of nothing but lace and satin lingerie. Whatever else had happened while he was lost to the world, woman's fashions had certainly gotten more interesting.

He lifted his eyes to the mirror over her dresser, seeing himself for the first time. He usually crafted his image to suit the needs of the woman he was targeting, changing his appearance to become what they most desired in a man. It was instinctive, and yet as he gazed at his reflection he realized this time he had appeared as he truly was. He ran a hand over his brow and chuckled. *Well, almost as he truly was.* His instincts still had sense enough to hide the jet black horns that normally rose from his hairline and curved back into dark hair. Some things a woman just wouldn't understand.

There was very little else in the room, no mementos and only a few feminine touches; a painting of a vibrant meadow on one wall, a portrait of an older woman set in a silver frame on the dresser, and little more. This woman was not someone who needed material things. Alistair took one last look around the room before shifting again, returning to the void. He remembered her nightmare and the pain he'd sensed when he touched her thoughts. No, whatever Keri yearned for in her life, it wasn't tied to money or objects. Given she was now the only hope he had of breaking free, he'd have to find out what she needed and offer it to her in exchange for his freedom.

* * * *

It had totally slipped her mind that Saturday was market day in Ganges, and Keri spent several happy hours wandering from stall to stall, sampling bits of this and that and speaking to the artists and farmers who had gathered to sell their wares.

She had forgotten how much fun it was to wander, and several times the artisans had recognized her, welcoming her back to the island. Two of them had helped teach Keri how to carve wood when she was a girl, and they both expressed hopes she'd reopen her grandmother's workshop and continue the family tradition. Though she had made them no promises, it helped her to know she'd be welcome back to the fold if she did take up the family craft again.

It was late afternoon when she drove home, her car laden down with food, some new crockery and the most beautiful tapestry she'd ever seen. The hand-spun yarn had been knotted and woven to create a stretch of wild and lonely seashore.

The waves seemed almost ready to crash down at any moment on the rocks that rose up out of the surf. Arbutus trees framed the shoreline, their trunks twisted by the wind into strange, stunted shapes. When Keri had bought it the weaver had told her it was inspired by a real beach on the island and had given her directions, assuring her it was worth the trek down through the woods to find.

It had taken several trips to get all her purchases into the house, and Keri laughed at herself as she eyed the heaps of food she'd bought. "Enough to feed an army, what was I thinking?" She busied herself finding room for it all, stuffing both the fridge and the pantry before she was done.

Inspired by her purchases, she cooked one of her grandmother's favorite recipes, a simple but savory casserole that filled the whole house with its fragrance and reminded her of times long past. Still feeling energized, she baked two raspberry crumbles, leaving them to cool on the counter top as she tucked into her dinner.

"A few weeks of this and you're going to need to buy a treadmill!" She poked at the soft curve of her stomach and shook her head. "Or a whole new wardrobe, something with elastic waistbands and the dimensions of a pup tent."

By ten o'clock she was nestled into a hot bubble bath with her second glass of wine, the scent of molten beeswax blending with the night blooming jasmine that grew outside the bathroom window. She dozed in the tub, her mind replaying the amazingly detailed dream she'd had that afternoon.

He'd had black hair that curled down to brush the top of the finest pair of shoulders she had ever seen, falling into his eyes in a way that made her fingers itch to sweep it to one side. A dusting of dark hairs covered his chest, tapering down over a well defined six pack to the largest cock she'd ever seen. *Definitely a dream man*, she laughed to herself as she let the warm water and wine do their magic.

Her hands drifted in the water, stroking her breasts absently as she remembered the way her dream lover's mouth had sucked on them, the memory of his tongue on her nipples drawing them into tight nubs all over again.

New fantasies replaced memory and Keri could almost feel male hands stroking down her body, her dream lover's mouth replacing her fingers as she played with herself. Her hands stroked down her body just as she had imagined his would, her thighs easing open as she arched her hips up, needing to ease the sexual tension that suddenly had her wound tight. She closed her eyes as her fingers slid into her sex, letting her imagination make them feel stronger, thicker than hers, a man's hand pleasuring her, his fingers circling her clitoris. Her hips jerked and she whispered Alistair's name, her fingers moving faster now.

Her orgasm came on gently, flooding her body with warmth and pleasure as her fingers worked over her clit one last time and she sighed with pleasure, feeling her tension ease again. As she lay there her imagination kicked in once again and she could have sworn she heard a man whisper the words "I want you."

That made her sit up, lifting her head and looking around her to try and find the source of the voice. "That's one very realistic fantasy you've been having." She settled back into the water slowly, withdrawing her hand from between her legs with a rueful laugh. "Now stop thinking about that non-existent, utterly gorgeous dream man and get out of this tub before you prune."

* * * *

From his prison Alistair had been watching, having sensed her return hours before. Her energy had danced on the edge of his awareness, coming and going from the magical boundaries that kept him captive.

He had planned to wait for her to drift off to sleep before he tried to contact her again, but as Keri lay in her warm bath he was able to sense her drowsy arousal. It tempted him to change his plans.

She was near enough to the bed he had been able to slip into her mind, and when he had he was pleased to discover her thoughts had all been of him. He'd built on her memories of their dream encounter, teasing her with images of his mouth on her breasts, lapping at her wet skin. While she was awake he couldn't accomplish much more than suggestion, but while she was receptive like this he couldn't resist enhancing her pleasure until she dreamed again and he could make it real.

Her orgasm had been a sensual treat, a tantalizing promise of what was to come. He'd been so intent on the pleasure he had felt that he missed the moment when she began to wake up fully, and in his hurry to withdraw from her mind he'd let his yearning for her be heard. Her reaction had pleased him, and he let himself return to the void with confidence that very soon he'd be strong enough to show her just how real he was. He found himself looking forward to that moment, very much.

His mind followed her as she crawled into bed without bothering with pajamas, her tired but contented thoughts coming through clearly as she settled down and closed her eyes in preparation for sleep. Her last words were a prayer he knew would be answered. "If it's not too much bother, I'd like to dream about him again, please."

After that, she had fallen asleep quickly, and he had wasted no time in slipping into her mind and arranging her dreams to his liking. He'd kept the image of her bedroom, adding candles to fill the area with soft light, and roses summoned up roses in crystal vases to sit on both sides of the bed. Finally he added himself to her dreams, appearing in bed beside her, his arms already reaching for her.

"You came back," she greeted him, coming into his arms willingly.

"Of course I came back. You asked for me to return." He turned his head and brushed a trail of kisses down her forearm. "What sort of man would refuse a beautiful woman such a request?"

"I can think of quite a few actually..." she started to argue he laid his fingers across her lips, stopping her words.

"Any man who failed to accept an invitation back to your bed is a fool." He informed her as he lowered her to the bed and moved above her, dropping a kiss to her lips. Alistair groaned as he kissed her again, drawing her full lower lip into his mouth. His free hand slid between them to cup her breast, teasing at her nipple with his thumb until it tightened in arousal.

Caged by his body, Keri could only writhe beneath his warm weight, one bare leg curling over the back of his thigh. As he released her lower lip she tangled her hands in his hair and drew him down into an open mouthed kiss, her tongue seeking his as she tasted him in turn.

"This feels so real." She whispered between kisses. He felt her try to focus, to try to understand and so he went about distracting her. His hands kneaded at her breasts, his kiss grew more demanding and then he moved atop her, his knee pressing between her thighs, opening her legs. He sensed her confusion fade as she accepted the dream, all other thoughts seared away by a newly kindled blaze of desire. Desire for him.

He ended their kiss with a gentle nip and then moved down her body, kneeling between her thighs so he could look over the beauty displayed on the bed before him. "Beautiful." He told her as she lifted her hands to reach for him. He gently brushed her hands away and then scooped her legs over his shoulders, lifting her body higher up the angle of his thighs as his lips and tongue found the sweet core of her sex.

His beautiful mortal mewled with surprise and pleasure at the sudden contact, her head falling back to the bed as she surrendered to the moment. He watched her fingers curl into the sheet, kneading at it as her hips bucked against his mouth in encouragement.

He held her in place firmly, his hands cradling the soft flesh of her buttocks, making sure that she could do nothing but submit to the pleasures he intended to give her.

His free hand moved between her thighs, gently teasing open her folds and exposing her clitoris. He ran his tongue over it, making her tremble as he slowly laved her most sensitive spots. Again and again his tongue swirled around her clit until her breathing grew ragged and she moaned his name.

"Please, I...I need..." She gasped and tensed her legs, trying to draw him closer. He laughed, every note vibrating against her slick folds as he lashed his tongue over her one more time and then drove it deep into her body, thrusting and teasing as she arched herself higher and finally came with a wild cry, the surge of energy that flowed between them filling him with power.

He let the dream go, allowing it to blur and slide sideways as it slowly faded back into the ether where it had been created. Frightened, Keri reached for him with a soft cry and he wrapped his arms around her, holding her to him as the dream ended. At that moment he shifted planes, materializing beside her on the bed. Now he held her as she slept, both of them bathed in moonlight.

It amazed him that she'd been aware of the shift, sensing when he'd left her dreams. She was more sensitive than he had suspected, which led to some rather interesting possibilities. His hands cupped a breast, feeling the warm weight of it. By Styx, she was amazing, even in the confines of her dreams she had released enough energy that he was nearly drunk with it.

He leaned down and brushed a kiss to her shoulder, reveling in the way her body melded to his as though she'd been made to his measure.

He'd take her soon, letting her wake from her dreams and into a reality where he was real and wanting her.

He knew that was the moment some turned from him, terrified of what he was and what he meant to their ordered understanding of the universe, but he was certain that Keri wouldn't fear him.

He'd lost so much in the centuries he'd been captive; time with family and friends, so many lost chances. The universe owed him this much at least, he wanted Keri and he'd do anything to keep her, anything to end the loneliness.

He let his hands drift over her body, learning every curve and line. She was more beautiful than her dreams had revealed, lush and soft and perfect. He nuzzled into her red hair, inhaling the scent of jasmine and her own sweet perfume. When she moaned and wiggled closer he bit back a groan as her ass pressed against his cock, already hard and growing harder with every passing moment. Dream sex was better than nothing, but it couldn't begin to reduce the need he felt for this woman, not after more than two centuries of being alone.

Gently he let one hand stroke down to her uppermost leg, coaxing it to drape over his thigh. As her thighs parted he could smell the scent of her arousal, tempting him to dip his fingers into her sweet honey and taste her. He let his fingers graze over her labia and she moaned again, her hips bucking against the light touch of his fingers. Even asleep she was a sensual creature, and Alistair knew taking her here, on this plane would be an unforgettable pleasure. He brought his fingers to his mouth and sucked on them, savoring her essence before returning them to her sex, gliding over her slick folds until he knew she was ready for him.

Keri woke slowly, the delicious sensations coming from her sex impossible to ignore. She felt thick pressure and opened her eyes just as her dream lover arched his hips and pressed his cock into her heated core, claiming her an inch at a time.

She gasped as he filled her, then panic clamped around her chest and choked her as she realized she was no longer dreaming.

Alistair held her close, not moving as he whispered in her ear. "It's me Keri, just me." He flashed her a smile as she twisted her head to stare up at him in shock and confusion.

"Alistair ?" Fear warred with amazement as she tried to make sense of what was happening. Her dream lover was behind her, making love to her, but she wasn't asleep anymore.

"Aye, Keri. I'm here." He leaned over to brush a tender kiss to her lips.

"But you can't be here, you're not real."

"Now that's where you're wrong my beauty." He shifted his hips, moving his cock deeper inside her. "I'm real, and I'm here, and I want to see you come undone in my arms again."

She met his gaze, dazzled by the desire that made his eyes glow like amber in sunlight. "But how?"

"I will answer all your questions soon." He kissed her again. "But right now I have a powerful need for you. Be with me Keri, please."

His *please* sent a tremor through her and she knew she couldn't deny his request, not when she wanted him so much it was nearly painful.

"Yes." She kissed him back, her pelvis already arching back to meet his next thrust.

With that single word he seemed to give himself free rein, driving his cock deep inside her with a growl of pleasure. His fingers parted her labia, seeking out her clitoris as he slammed into her again.

She squirmed, barely able to breathe as his cock filled and stroked her in ways she had never even imagined.

She had never felt so mastered, Alistair's strong body curving around hers and laying claim to it while she could do nothing but try to stay above the tidal waves of sensation he sent crashing through her. Just as her final shreds of control started to slip he withdrew and she keened in displeasure at the loss.

"Patience little one." He laughed as his strong hands tugged at her hips and guided her to her hands and knees. She lowered her head and raised her hips in an open invitation as she felt him kneel behind her, but instead of thrusting into her he caged her body with his and buried his face into her hair, showering kisses over her shoulders and back. She could feel his rock hard length resting between her thighs and she moaned in frustration, wiggling herself against him in protest at his delay.

"What do you want Keri?" His voice was a breathless tickle at her ear, the faint burr of his accented words adding to her longing.

"You." She answered and turned her head to kiss him.

"As my lady wishes." He took her again, burying himself so deep inside her that there was no room between their bodies. She felt her inner walls grip him hard and Alistair groaned loudly, thrusting into her over and over until they were both hovering on the edge of control.

Keri reached between her legs and pinched her clit, bringing herself to climax on a scream.

Her body's release triggered Alistair's and he followed her into ecstasy with a shuddering roar as his balls emptied themselves in her womb.

Panting, he tugged her back into his arms as he lay back on the bed, dragging the sheet over them both. Keri snuggled into his side without protest, her red hair fanned out over his shoulder as she laid her head on his chest. Her fingers traced over the ridged lines of his stomach and she laughed softly. "You certainly feel real."

"As do you." He twined a lock of her hair around a calloused finger. "Did you think that somehow I'd vanish in a puff of smoke when we were done?"

She laughed at him and turned her head to watch his fingers as they played with her hair. "I don't know. Can you even do that? Vanish that is? Or do you just wander into random women's dreams and then appear in their beds? And how is it that you know my name?"

"So many questions, where do I begin?" He lifted his head to grin at her briefly before laying back once more. "I know your name because I have been inside your mind and touched your thoughts. I can't conjure smoke, but I suppose I could vanish if I chose to, at least it would seem to you that I vanished. And to answer the question you haven't asked yet, my trusting and sweet Keri, I am no threat to you, I swear it."

Keri raised herself on one elbow and gazed down at him. "I think I'm going to need something to drink to get through this conversation. Would you care to join me?"

"It's been a very long time since I've enjoyed food or drink, I'd be happy to join you."

She kissed his cheek and left the bed, and he watched in appreciation as her curvy form walked away from him towards the door.

As she reached the threshold, she turned back and grinned. "I will only leave this room if you promise to still be here when I get back."

Alistair raised one hand off the bed and placed it over his heart. "You have my word Keri, I couldn't leave this bed if my life depended on it."

CHAPTER FOUR

Keri stood naked in her kitchen and tried to wrap her brain around what had just happened. The most gorgeous man she'd ever seen had just stepped out of her dreams and into her bed, and she'd enjoyed every wanton, amazing minute of it. She never did things like this, ever. She pinched her arm sharply and winced at the sting. Well, at least I'm not still dreaming.

She gathered up her wits and set about making a midnight snack for them both; red wine, fresh bread and some of the cheeses she'd bought at the market that afternoon. Setting it all on a tray, she carried it back into her bedroom, her cheeks heating as she realized that in her daze she'd never put on as much as a bathrobe.

He had remade the bed while she was gone, folding the heavier blankets at the foot board and stacking up enough pillows for them to lie back on.

The sheet was pulled up to his waist, leaving his upper torso bare to her gaze and he grinned as he patted the bed beside him. "Bring that over here and I'll answer your questions as we eat."

She placed the tray between them and snatched the first thing she could find out of her lingerie drawer, stifling a groan as she realized the concoction of cream lace and satin she'd blindly grabbed was more enticement than camouflage.

Keri joined him on the bed and tugged up the sheet as quickly as she could, trying to ignore the flash of amusement in Alistair's eyes as he took in her outfit and actions.

"You're beautiful Keri, but if you insist on covering up that beauty, I'm glad you chose this." He reached out and brushed his knuckles over the lace covering her breasts.

She felt her cheeks heat and ducked her head, struggling to focus on pouring the wine instead of how much that single caress affected her.

"I've got that." He took the glass from her trembling fingers and poured them each a generous measure. Watching her over the rim of his glass he suddenly asked, "Are you afraid of me?"

"No. Well, maybe. Not of you, but of all of this. It's just a lot to take in, and I don't understand what's happened. I'm here having a glass of wine with a figment of my imagination, it's all very damned weird."

She took a drink of her wine and tried to calm herself. "What are you, and why are you here?"

Alistair took a sip of the wine and flashed her a comforting smile that made her heart skip a beat. "I am an incubus, what you would call a demon, and I am here because about two hundred years ago a cold-hearted bitch of a sorceress cast a spell that imprisoned me." He reached out and knocked on the carved headboard. "I'm bound to this bed until I find a way to break the spell."

"You're a demon?" Fear flared deep inside her, and she tensed as she tried to decide which way to bolt.

He nodded. "Yes, but that doesn't make me evil" He lifted a hand to reach out for her, touching her hand with the gentlest of caresses.

"I've already given you my word I'll not harm you. It pains me to see fear in your eyes, just let me explain."

She downed a goodly portion of her wine and then nodded in consent. "Alright, explain."

"You know of demons, so I imagine you know of angels too?" She gave him a slight nod, and he continued. "We're really the same race, but we have differing needs. We call ourselves daemons. In simple terms, what you think of as angels feed on the light side of the emotional spectrum, while demons feed on the dark side. We're not like humans; we live on energy, not food and water, though we can enjoy both. Different types of daemons feed on different energies. Angels feed on the higher emotions like love and courage, while demons feed on other, more primal emotions like anger, fear, pain, and...." His voice lowered, and he let his gaze wander over her lace covered cleavage as he added, "Lust."

"So you're a lust demon? Seriously?" Keri's shoulders hunched forward, and her eyes lowered to the tray of food. Inside her head, the negative voices began to taunt her. See? He doesn't want you; you're just the woman who happened to buy the bed he's trapped in. He didn't choose you; you're the only meal on the menu.

"Incubus." He corrected her, concern showing on his face as she lowered her gaze. "I can only feed on the sexual energy of the woman I am with."

"That explains why you look like sin incarnate; you'd have to be to get what you need to live." Keri popped a cube of Havarti into her mouth, her eyes still downcast.

"We have the ability to change our appearance, to become that which our partner most desires. It's something all of my daemon type can do, along with touching another's thoughts or dream walking." Alistair set down his glass and reached out to cup Keri's chin, his thumb grazing her lips as he coaxed her to lift her head.

"Why are you hurting? I can feel your pain without even entering your mind."

"I'm a goose, it's nothing."

She finally lifted her head to meet his gaze, her green eyes carefully shuttered to hide any emotion.

"I can take the information from your mind, or you can tell me yourself, but either way Keri, I am going to know what has upset you."

"I'm an idiot, that's all. I should have known that the most amazing, handsome man I've ever met wasn't really interested in me. I'm just the only woman around, and you needed to feed." She turned crimson at her confession and turned her face away from his caress, downing the rest of her wine in a few short swallows.

He stared at her in obvious surprise and then shook his head. "You're not an idiot, and I am not only with you because I needed to feed." Ignoring the tray between them he reached over and hauled Keri bodily into his lap, cradling her close.

"I sensed you days ago, the first time I'd sensed anything in so long I thought I had finally gone mad. Your energy woke me, and I called out to you. You must have heard me, Beautiful, for here I am, awake and corporeal. I'm only here because of you."

"I felt something," Keri admitted softly, her back tingling where his hands smoothed up and down her spine, soothing her. "I heard something like a voice, only it was too quiet, and then I found the bed, and when I touched it, I heard it again. I knew I had to have the bed, bring it home and restore it." She let her head sink into the cradle of his shoulder, her cheek on his chest.

He kept up his caresses and her body responded, softening and melting a little at a time as his voice rumbled by her ear. "You saved me, Keri. Daemons are more or less immortal barring violence, but only if we have the will to continue. I was nearly lost when you found me."

"I'm glad I found you. I've been a bit lost myself lately, it's a horrible feeling."

"Neither of us is lost anymore." He threaded his fingers through her hair and tipped back her head to steal a gentle kiss from her lips. "Now, where was I? Oh yes, daemons aren't all bad, and you think I look like sin incarnate."

"Which makes sense, since you can look like whoever I think is the sexiest." She gave him a half smile and offered him a morsel of cheese. "Now, the question is why you look like that, and not like Gerard Butler."

"I don't know who that is, but as it turns out, this is my true form. The transformation is instinctive, I don't control it. But right now you're looking at the real me. I've never had that happen before."

"You're perfect," Keri informed him and pressed a light kiss to his chin. "So you're what my ideal man looks like? No wonder I've never found him. And I thought demons were all pointy ears and tails and horns? Or is that all wrong too?"

Alistair laughed. "There are many different types of daemons, and yes, some of them have very strange and often terrifying appearances. Would you still think I'm perfect if I had pointy ears or horns?"

"I suspect it would take more than a tail, or Mr. Spock ears to mess with your looks."

"Good." He scooped another morsel from the tray, this time feeding her. "Then one day I may show you my horns."

"Wait, you actually have horns? Keri nearly choked as she spluttered in shock. "Oh, now you have to show me."

* * * *

Alistair found he was enjoying himself, laughing and teasing the beautiful woman in his lap. There had been women who had invited him into their lives before but he'd never wanted to do so.

He had always craved pleasure and sex, not laughter and flirtation. He set those thoughts aside with a mental wave of the hand. He'd been alone too long, that was all.

"If I show you my horns, what will you do for me? Hmm?"

Keri appeared to consider his question for a moment before making her offer. "I'll show you my world."

"You can't do that, for I cannot go more than five paces from this accursed bed. The world is denied to me Keri, both yours and mine."

"Well, I can't help you with your world, but I can help you explore mine. Things have changed since last you were here, and I think I know a way. But first you owe me the rest of your story, and I still haven't seen these horns."

"How can such a pretty little thing be so demanding?" Very well, I agree to your terms." Alistair leaned down and slanted his lips over hers, kissing her until they were both breathless. When he lifted his lips from hers, she opened her eyes and gasped softly.

"Horns." She murmured in amazement and lifted a hand, pausing it near his cheek.

"May I?" He nodded and she brushed her fingertips over one, her gentle exploration sending a bolt of heat straight to his groin.

"They're the same color as your hair," she observed as she let her fingers continue exploring, following the curve until it ended in a sharp point almost lost in his dark hair. "I don't think you're perfect anymore. Now I've seen these, I think you're smoking hot."

Laughter rumbled up from his chest, and he felt a rush of satisfaction flow through him as he leaned in and whispered. "I take it that's a good thing?"

"A very, very good thing."

"I'm glad you like them. I've never let one of your kind see them before. No mortal but you has ever seen me as I truly am."

"I'm honored," she finished her examination and flashed him a pleased smile. "It seems odd, but now I really believe you're a dem— er, daemon and not just a very strange man."

She settled herself deeper into his lap and let her head rest on his shoulder again. "Now, how did you get here?"

"My father is a powerful daemon, and I was the first son born to him in a millennium. He made sure I lacked for nothing and was given the best teachers and training he could arrange. I mastered the art of shifting between planes when I was still young, only a hundred or so years old. I reveled in my abilities and spent the next century exploring every part of your world, growing stronger but not much wiser. That's when Cora sent her summons and captured me. I had been warned time, and again that human sorcerers were dangerous, too powerful for all but the strongest of us to face alone. The spell she acted like a lure, and I foolishly thought I could handle her. I was wrong, and she kept me for her entertainment for another hundred years before she disappeared, and I was left alone."

"For her entertainment? You mean you and she—" Keri trailed off and gestured vaguely to the bed.

He shook his head in the negative. "If she had let me get that close to her I'd have killed her with my bare hands. Using me that way might have been her initial plan, but when she realized how angry I was, she simply enforced all the spells binding me and kept me alive as a pet. She was a sorceress, and she'd found a way to feed off of sexual energy in a way similar to a daemon, only she used the energy to power her spells and to keep herself young and beautiful. Because of that, she surrounded herself with sex. While I was her prisoner she ran brothels and pleasure houses, leeching energy off of every depraved act."

Keri wrapped her arms around his chest and hugged him, "I'm so sorry. That must have been hard to face every day."

"She perverted everything we are and twisted it into something cruel and ugly.

If I ever get free of this prison, I will do everything in my power to hunt her down and destroy her for all she's done."

He fought back the wave of anger and pain as he tried to deal with the memories of his capture, burying his face into Keri's soft curls and inhaling her sweet fragrance until he felt he was calm enough to continue.

"If it's too hard, you don't need to tell me anything more."

Alistair realized they had changed roles, now she was comforting him, her hands stroking him just as he had done for her. Not since he'd left his mother's home had anyone cared for him like this. It was another thing Cora had stolen from him, time with the friends and family he loved, and who loved him. So long as his personal gate to his home plane of Daemos stood, they knew he lived, but where he was or what he had been through, none of them knew or could know until he freed himself and returned home.

"No, I promised you I would explain it all, and I will." Alistair's voice was low and rough as he nuzzled her hair again. "I just have not had another soul to tell this to before."

Keri encouraged him to continue, "So she was a madam, surrounding herself with sex all the time to stay young. So why did she keep you? I don't understand."

"I was something of a pet to her, an amusement. But I could also be used to give her powerful doses of energy. She would starve me, leave me alone until I was too weak to resist, and then she'd bring in a woman, some bored wife or socialite's daughter who wanted a night of rough and ready sex with no witnesses or risk of discovery. They paid richly for the privilege of spending a night with me. I didn't desire them, but being starved of energy is unpleasant, and I would have done anything to ease my hunger."

He paused and shifted her in his lap so he could hold her even closer.

"She always watched my encounters, in the room but far enough away she knew I could not reach her. She would let me take their essence, but she would steal part of mine as well, enough to keep me weakened.

I think it was like a drug to her, absorbing so much energy at once."

"Then what happened? You said she vanished one day, why?" Keri's fingers slid through his dark hair, smoothing back the lock that fell into his eyes. "She kept you prisoner for all those years, and then just abandoned you?"

"Her business would always be discovered eventually. Usually, she would be careful enough that it took years to come to the authority's attention, and years more before the bribes stopped working. I think she got careless, or someone more politically powerful than she went after her. I only overheard bits and snippets of conversations and thoughts, most of it happened outside the small sphere I am bound to. There was a raid, arrests were made, and Cora fled the city. The property sat idle for a long time, but eventually, the city sold it. By then I had been too long without feeding, and I'm not really sure what happened. I drifted in a void, too weak to shift to this plane and too stubborn to give up and die, at least not right away."

"If I had you prisoner in my bed, I'd never have left you behind." She gave him a half smile and kissed the corner of his mouth. "You're amazing."

He felt a stab of sadness as she smiled up at him, her green eyes so gentle. She didn't understand, not yet. "But you do have me, prisoner, my beauty. The bed belongs to you, and I am bound to the bed." He gathered her small hands in his larger ones and cradled them near his chest. "My life is in your hands."

Keri's mouth formed an "O" and tears sparkled in her lovely dark green eyes. "I don't want to keep you prisoner. If we found a way to free you, what would you do?"

Alistair's voice was a low growl when he answered, his words roughened by emotion. "I'd go home. My family is waiting for me there, my life is there.

When I return home, I will gather my family together, and we'll hunt down Cora and destroy her if she still survives."

Keri spoke so softly her words were more breath than sound, "I'd miss you."

Her next words were rushed as if she were trying to talk over what she had just confessed "If there's a way to free you, we'll find it. I don't know anything about magic or daemons, but I will help any way I can. And this is the first time you've been free to go over the bed without someone interfering. Maybe we'll find something that was missed before."

"Aye, maybe we will." Back in control of his emotions, Alistair gave her a grin. "But before we worry about breaking enchantments and such, I'll need to be stronger." Amusement and desire gleamed in his eyes as he stared into Keri's. "Do you think you can help me with that?"

Keri laughed and twined her arms around his neck. "Oh, I imagine I could. Just how much stronger do you need to be before you can try to free yourself?"

His grin grew wicked, and he lowered his lips to hers, punctuating his words with heated kisses. "Much, much, much, stronger. It could take ages to get there."

"Such a hardship this will be." She laughed in answer.

CHAPTER FIVE

Keri was in her kitchen taking stock of her morning's work: bacon, eggs, fresh cured ham steaks and hash browns had all been prepared in the hour since she'd woken up. Feeling achy and well loved, she'd left Alistair sleeping and grabbed a hot shower, basking in the heat as it eased muscles she hadn't known she had until last night. She was full of energy this morning, despite getting only a few hours of sleep between rounds of the most amazing sex she'd ever had. When not even her singing in the shower had woken her sleeping lover, she'd decided to cook him breakfast.

"I think you got a bit carried away." She laughed at herself as she eyed the counter full of food. She'd also brewed coffee, adding to her energy level as the caffeine hit her system.

Not sure how daemons preferred their coffee, she tossed milk and sugar onto the tray and went to lift it, then set it back down. "Well hell, that's not going to work." She pondered for a moment and then grinned and headed for the bedroom.

She entered quietly and then smiled as she noticed him watching her from beneath dark lashes. "Good morning."

Alistair left the bed, gathering her up in his arms and kissing her senseless. "Now it's a wonderful morning."

It took her a moment to register anything other than the rush of heat that flowed through her the moment his lips touched hers, but as he lifted his head to let her catch her breath she took in his height, stunned to realize he towered over her five foot three frame by more than a foot at least. He made her feel positively petite as he held her.

As her fingers smoothed over his chest, she also realized he had gotten dressed. "How— where did you find clothes?" She leaned back to see him better and saw that his shirt was fastened with ties, not buttons, and his pants were a soft fabric she didn't recognize.

His lips curved into a smile. "There are advantages to being a daemon."

"I'll say there are. So can you dress in anything you can imagine? Or are you conjuring this up from some magical closet back in your own plane of existence?"

"No closet, this is part of the same ability that lets me change my appearance."

"Nice trick, if I could do that I'd save a fortune on clothes." Keri fingered the fabric curiously, then remembered why she'd come into the bedroom.

"If you like I thought we could eat outside. There's a deck just through the french doors, and its close enough you would be able to sit out there. I just need to ask one really stupid question." She gestured outside. "Sunlight isn't going to make you dissolve or turn to dust or anything, is it?

Alistair burst out laughing and shook his head. "I'm not a vampire thank you, I'm an *incubus*! I don't run around sucking blood, that's disgusting."

"Well I don't have my Demonology guide handy, how was I to know?"

Keri's cheeks heated and shooed him out of her way so she could open the doors, letting the morning breeze in. The room instantly filled with the scent of lavender and growing things. A small glass and wrought iron table sat out on the cedar deck, accompanied by several matching chairs.

You grab a chair, and I'll go get breakfast." As she headed for the door, she glanced back and said, "And I'm glad you're not a vampire.

I'm not sure I'd be willing to let you suck me dry just to get your strength back."

She could hear him laughing all the way back to the kitchen.

Coming back, she watched as Alistair paced out the distance carefully, looking pleased as he walked what she assumed must be the limits of his prison. When she moved again, he came to meet her, taking the overloaded tray from her the moment he saw how much she was carrying. "I have that, I'm sorry I can't of more help." His golden brown eyes showed regret and a flash of irritated pride as he set the tray down and pulled out a chair for her to sit in.

"It's alright, I understand. You just did more than my husband did in all the years we were together, thank you."

She sat gracefully and tucked an errant curl behind her ear before gesturing to the tray. "I know I made an awful lot of food given I'm on a diet, and you don't even need to eat, but I like to cook, and I haven't had anyone to cook for in a long time."

"We do not need to eat, but we still enjoy it. Everything looks wonderful, and you should not be on a diet." Alistair's eyes rove over her body, his desire for her very evident in his gaze. "You are beautiful Keri, any man who thinks otherwise is a fool. All women have their own unique beauty, it has been a source of never-ending confusion to my kind that mortal men fail to see this. It's why we have prospered on this plane, there are so many women unclaimed or neglected by their men."

He filled a plate with food and handed it to Keri before filling one of his own.

"You said you had a husband, do you not have one anymore?"

Keri took the plate with a bemused smile and pushed a mug of coffee towards him. "He decided he wanted a newer model." She quipped and then stopped as she saw his confused expression.

"He divorced me to be with someone new, a woman much younger and prettier than I am." She explained as she poured a dollop of milk into her coffee and sipped it. "We were married just over ten years, and he walked away from it all as if none of it mattered like I never mattered. At least he was fair; the settlement gave me more than enough to live on for the rest of my life. To get it, all I had to do was stay quiet and not fight the divorce. I guess he'd be one of those men you said your kind doesn't understand."

She shrugged slightly, trying to keep her voice light and hide the pain that still rose up when she thought about Brent and what had happened. "You said you prospered on this plane, does that mean there are others?"

"I'm sorry Keri, I didn't mean to cause you upset." His hand reached across the small table to brush a tear from her cheek. "To answer your question, yes, there are other planes; a great many others. Some are much like this one, some are wildly different, and all have their beauties and their dangers. Some are certain death for my kind, and others, like yours, are similar enough that some elders believe long ago our species were closely related, two planes that intersected or developed in parallel. No one is sure how or why, but as far as I know your race is one of very few that can bear children of mixed blood, human and daemon."

Keri blinked and set down the forkful of egg she had been about to eat. "What? We can have children? I could have your baby?"

"My kind does not often conceive children, but yes, it is possible."

"You knew that and you— we didn't use any protection! You should have warned me! I was barely able to think last night with everything that happened, but you knew!" Keri pushed back from the table, hurt and anger twisting like serpents in her stomach.

"You are not fertile right now; there was no risk of a child." Alistair left his seat and came around to crouch beside her, his hand on her thigh. "This body is not like yours Keri, I carry no disease. I swore to you last night I would not harm you, and I meant that. You are the only being in all the planes I can talk to, I would never hurt you." His gaze met hers, "I'm sorry I said what I did. I could have handled that much better."

She knew her cheeks were red from the heat in them, and she could feel the tears that stung her eyes, but she managed to take a slow breath and as she crammed all her lost dreams for a family back into their box and mentally slammed the lid closed again.

"I'm sorry I reacted so badly, It's just that I haven't been with anyone since my divorce, and it only now occurred to me how reckless I was last night." She reached out, her fingers brushing over his brow and stroking the horns he had left unhidden. "We're going to find a way to free you and then you're going to go back to your family. I'm not sure I'd be up for raising a half-demon baby all alone."

"Children born to my kind and yours are called cambions. They are mortal but have many of the abilities of their daemonic parent.

81

Sorcerers, seers, and other psychics among your kind are almost always cambions or their descendants. The gifts vary depending on the type of daemon involved." Alistair turned his head and brushed a kiss to her wrist. "If it were to happen, Keri, I would never leave you to raise my child alone. I give you my word."

"How do you know you haven't already left children behind to be raised by their mothers?"

"I would know, it is part of what I am. We know when our bloodline has been continued. You are not pregnant, and I have never been given the gift of fatherhood. I was the first son to be born to my father in a thousand years, my House values our children above all else because they are so rare."

"Brent, my ex-husband, always told me he wanted children someday. He knew I wanted a family, but he went and had a vasectomy in secret, kept it hidden from me for years. It was only when I wanted to look into fertility treatments, convinced that there was something wrong with *me* that he finally confessed."

"He had something done to stop him from fathering children?" Alistair's voice was full of outrage and horror. "He did this deliberately and then hid it from you? What sort of man does this?"

"He was a selfish ass who didn't want anything or anyone to mess up his perfect life." Keri couldn't hide the hurt and anger she was feeling, but even as she felt it rise within her, she realized it was less than it had been before. In a moment of intuition, she leaned down and kissed Alistair, passionate and tender at the same time. "He's nothing at all like you."

Her words seemed to affect him deeply, and Alistair made a low noise of need as he gathered her close, hauling her off the chair and against his chest. Their meal, their conversation all forgotten but as they kissed again and again.

She tangled her fingers into his hair and laughed as he overbalanced and they both landed in a tangled heap on the deck, Keri sprawled on top of him. Even as they fell she sensed him positioning himself so that his body cushioned hers and he held her close, protecting her.

"Breakfast is up there," Laughter burbled up inside her, and she found herself grinning. "So why are we down here?"

Strong hands cupped her cheeks, and he drew her down to kiss her again. "You kissed me, and we ended up here. This is entirely your doing."

"My fault? The big strong daemon is going to blame the itty-bitty mortal woman for this?" She teased him, her cheeks flushed with laughter.

"Aye, I am. And if you keep protesting your innocence I may keep you down here until breakfast is cold."

"Oh no, we don't want to do that. Well, maybe we do, but if that happens then I won't get around to showing you the world for hours, and I suspect you'd like to see what you've been missing." Keri beamed. "So, what's it going to be?"

Alistair groaned at having to choose, "Can't we do both?" Even as he complained he sat up and lifted her up and off his body, settled her gently on the deck beside him. He then leaned in to steal another kiss before standing up and helping her to her feet.

"Very well then, first we will break our fast, then you will show me the world, and then my beautiful Keri, I am going to pleasure you out here in the garden." He pulled out her seat and guided her into it before taking his own. "Does this meet with your approval?"

She met his eyes from across the table and nodded. "It's a wonderful plan."

* * * *

Alistair indulged himself with the meal, savoring every mouthful as he enjoyed Keri's quiet company and the unadulterated joy of being corporeal and free of the void. After they had eaten, she had taken his hand and led him to the bathroom. More than anything else, this room was a stark reminder of how long he had been away. Hot water at the turn of a tap, sweet smelling soaps and lotions all neatly stored in their bottles and boxes, even the massive mirror that claimed much of one wall, these were great luxuries in the time he'd come from. "Are you wealthy?"

She stood up, a toothbrush still encased in some sort of clear wrapping in one hand and a clean washcloth in the other. "What? Wealthy? Not really. Why?" She handed him the items and gave him a puzzled look.

"It's hard to imagine everyone lives this way now. Things have changed so much. When I was last on this plane, only someone of great wealth could have afforded such luxury." He gestured around them.

"You'll get used to it." She murmured and kissed his cheek tenderly. "I'll help you."

After she had gone, he could still hear her out in the bedroom, clearing away the remains of the meal she had cooked for him. As he washed his face, he let his fingers linger where she had kissed his cheek, and he wondered why a woman of Keri's sweet nature and gentle beauty remained alone in the world.

He examined the shower but opted to postpone using it until he could convince Keri to join him. Grinning at the image of the two of them entangled under a stream of hot water, he stepped back into the bedroom and blinked at the changes she'd wrought in a short time.

Keri gestured for him to join her by the bed. "It's not exactly top of the line technology, but I've brought the television and DVD player in here, and I'm just going to set up my laptop in a moment. Fortunately, I convinced my grandmother to join the modern world a few years ago, so we have Internet access and even wifi."

Alistair felt as though Keri were speaking in a strange new language. "Wifi? DVD? You are speaking in riddles woman. What is all this?"

She beamed at him, "This is how I am going to show you the world. Now you go get comfy on the bed, and I'll be able to show you what I mean in just a minute."

Alistair sprawled out on the bed, a spike of lust spearing through him as she bent over to plug in the laptop cabling, giving him a view of her sweetly curved ass.

"There are so many things I could be exploring while lying on this bed. Are you sure you want to start with this Internet contraption?"

She ignored his suggestion with a laugh and continued fiddling with cables until a chirp and a flashing light made her crow with success. She carried the laptop back to the bed and set it down between them. "If we don't stick to the plan now, I suspect it will be hours before we remember what the plan even was."

"Well, that is likely true." He idly ran a hand down the curve of her hip, but his eyes were already on the laptop screen. "So what is this little wonder?"

Keri took his hand and placed it over the external mouse, showing him how to move the cursor, her fingers lying atop his as she taught him the basic elements of computer navigation. At first, he struggled, not with the concept, but with the shifts in language and spelling since last he'd attempted to read on this plane.

Soon, he had mastered enough to grasp the gist of the information presented to him, a veritable flood of history, politics, war and advancement that spanned his entire absence.

Keri stayed at his side for the next two hours, her soft voice coaching him through the more difficult passages, helping him to make sense of what he was seeing, keeping him grounded when he felt overwhelmed by it all.

When his eyes glazed over from his efforts to focus she shut down the laptop and turned on the television. Fascinated, he played with the remote, flipping channels and altering the volume over and over again. "That is why men don't get control of the remote control." She finally announced, laughing as she retrieved the device from his hand. "You're like a little boy in a candy shop! Just one show at a time Alistair or you'll make us both dizzy."

She selected a channel that specialized in science and discovery programs and left it playing, the volume quiet enough they could converse.

He pointed to the screen, where a narrator was describing the processing of some sort of frozen meals on a massive scale. "Your people have made great advancements while I was away, and yet you are still much as you were. I would never have imagined it."

"If you're tired of my world, you could tell me about yours. I want to know what it's like."

He flipped the television off and drew Keri into his arms, laying them both back into the pillows. One arm curled around her, holding her close while the other smoothed through her hair, coaxing her head to come down on his chest.

When her body was fitted to his, he felt a wave of contentment wash over him.

"We have many of the same things you do here, trees and lakes, mountains and seas that seem to go on forever. But there are many differences as well. The greatest difference, though, is what you would call magic. In Daemos, magic is part of everyday life, we are born to it. It is incorporated into our homes and cities; the land itself resonates with it. Here, there are only a few places where the magic seeps through, and only those with daemonic blood can wield it." He felt her stir against him, her arm slipping over his stomach to hold him.

"Would you take me there someday? When we find a way to free you?"

Alistair sighed, "I wish I could, but no one has found a way to bring your race through the veil that divides the planes. Only my kind and some of the known cambions can manage it. Attempting to shift planes is fatal to humans, it would kill you, beautiful girl."

"I see. I would have liked to see your world, but I guess that's just not to be." She lifted her head to look at him. "Is there a succubus waiting for you back there? Someone special?"

"You mean a mate?" He blinked, surprised at her question. "No, I hadn't taken a mate. I was still too young to have really considered it. If I hadn't been trapped here, I might have by now, but there was no woman I had found to capture my attention that way. And incubi do not mate with succubi; it's an almost impossible pairing."

Keri's brow furrowed. "Impossible? I would think it would be ideal. Both of you need the same thing to survive. Why doesn't it work?"

"If I were to bed a succubus, she would be feeding off of my pleasure while I fed off hers, but the longer it went on, the more we would drain from each other. It tends to end in two very exhausted daemons who have expended more energy than they gained." Alistair grinned at her. "When we are first learning to control our powers such pairings are actually encouraged, mostly because they keep young sex daemons too tired to molest the rest of the population. Such pairings are also always sterile, so if we wish to have children, we need to find mates outside our own daemon type."

"So one of your parents wasn't...what you are?"

"My father is an incubus, as I am. My mother is what you would call an angel. She feeds on feelings of love."

"Your mother is an *angel*? How does that even work?"

He laughed at her puzzled expression, burying his hand in her hair and tugging her head back for a kiss before answering her question. "Remember I told you, demons and angels are not the way you think of them. We are all daemons, a single race with many types. The world doesn't end if what you call a demon, and an angel share a bed, though I will confess there were those in both their Houses who were less than pleased about it.

My parents have been together for many centuries, but there are still those who do not approve of their mating. They have fights that could set the sky afire sometimes, but they have always found a way to cope with their differences.

I have half-siblings on both sides from previous pairings, brothers and sisters far older than I am. Near immortality makes a lifelong commitment a far greater challenge than for you mortals, so there are few among my kind who makes the choice to bind their souls to each other in a permanent mating. My parents chose to do so before I was born. They will be bound until death finds them, or time ends."

"They bound their souls? What does that mean?"

He answered by lifting her small hand and threading their fingers together, closing his hand around hers to lock them together. "It is more than a temporary pairing; it means that their two souls are linked together so tightly that nothing can part them. They can share everything they are with each other. There can be no secrets, no lies. And if one of them should be killed, the other will follow them into death, they cannot exist without each other."

Her fingers tightened around his, and she sighed softly. "It sounds amazing, and terrifying at the same time. Do you think you'd want to be bound that way? Or will you go back to the way it was before you were caught?"

"It is very rare for my daemon type to bind their soul to another. Temporary matings do happen, but they usually last only a century or two. I admire what my parents have, but I've never thought about it for myself. If my father is to be believed, though, the sex is so amazing it makes up for the lack of variety."

Keri's eyes widened, and she blushed bright pink. "Your father actually said that?"

"He did. He's a very outspoken fellow; it comes with his age and power. There are few who would argue with him, save for my mother. She is completely unimpressed by his power or his temper. Watching them together is a joy."

"I wish I had such memories of my family. I never knew my mother, and my father I don't really remember at all. He died in a car accident when I was young.

His mother, my Gran, raised me here in this house. I was always yearning to get away to the big city, to go live in Vancouver where things seemed so much more interesting."

Keri laughed softly, her eyes closing as she snuggled closer to him. "It took me a long time to finally come home, but I always was a slow learner."

She drifted off to sleep then, and Alistair cradled her close, letting her rest as he flipped on the television and let the information flow over him. He could feel the energy she had given him so freely surging through his body, rebuilding and revitalizing him.

He would let her sleep for now, but he could already sense his hunger for her body growing. Just thinking about her soft skin and the way she cried out his name in the thrall of her pleasure made his cock ache and his heart beat faster. She was as addictive as any drug. His gaze drifted over her sleeping form, and he brushed a stray lock of hair from her cheek. He had to find a way to break the spells soon. The longer he spent with Keri, the harder it was going to be to leave her.

CHAPTER SIX

When Keri woke up, her thoughts were all in a confused tangle. It was bright and sunny outside, and she wasn't alone in bed. It took her a moment to shake loose the cobwebs of sleep and remember everything that had happened since yesterday. She turned her head and opened her eyes to find herself lost in a pair of golden brown eyes that stared down into hers.

"Hello beautiful," Alistair greeted her with a smile just before his lips touched hers, sending sparks throughout her body.

"Now that's the best way to be woken up, ever." She kissed him back and laughed. "How long was I asleep?"

"Just an hour or so, you needed the rest." His grin turned wicked as his fingers slid underneath her shirt to cup one breast. "I thought it best I let you sleep, so you could be ready for the rest of my plans for today."

"And just what were those plans? My memory is a bit fuzzy on the details." She teased him as she basked in the flames of desire that flared in his eyes.

"I intend to remove these clothes, carry you back outside and have you out there on the deck." He pinched her nipple, making it harden beneath his fingers.

"And then when we're all hot and tousled from that, I am going to take you again, up against the wall of that shower you showed me earlier." Her skin flushed hot, and she moaned softly in response to his words.

"Oh yes, *that* plan." She wet her lips with the tip of her tongue and tried to remember to breathe. "I remember now." Keri's hands went to her jean's zipper and started to undo them, only to feel Alistair's hand release her breast and cover her hands, stopping her.

"I'll do it." He told her in a voice gone low and rough. He rolled off the bed and helped her up, standing her by the bed.

"Hands at your sides, no helping." He instructed her, his hands smoothing her sleep jumbled waves of hair back from her face. Alistair moved to stand behind her, his lips brushing the nape of her neck as his hands slid down her sides to take hold of the bottom of her t-shirt. He removed it slowly, letting his fingers brush over her breasts as he drew it higher.

"Lift your arms," he murmured near her ear. Keri complied, her heart racing as her arms reached over her head.

He tugged her shirt off and tossed it aside, drawing her hands back down to her sides before nuzzling his face into her hair. His hands came around to cup her breasts again, and she could feel the hard ridge of his cock pressing against her back. He shifted his hips, rubbing along her body. Warm breath feathered against her skin and Keri mewled in pleasure, surprising herself.

"You're enjoying this?" He asked as his lips brushed her throat.

"Mmhmm," she almost purred her response as warmth and desire flooded her body.

His thumbs circled her nipples in concert, drawing another small moan from her lips. She arched her back, arching her generous curves into his hands and swaying her hips to rub up against his crotch.

Alistair's mouth found her earlobe, sucking it into his mouth and nibbling on the edge. His fingers pinched her nipples lightly and then moved between them to undo the clasp of her bra. He brushed the straps down over her shoulders, releasing her breasts. "These are beautiful. If I had my way you would not bind them as you do."

Keri laughed and glanced down at her chest. "If I didn't, I'd bounce all over the place."

"Exactly." Alistair didn't hide his amusement at their conversation. "I could watch these bounce for hours." He ran his hands down her arms and over her stomach, stopping when he reached the tops of her jeans.

She let out a small gasp of breath as one hand slid lower, cupping her mound against his palm. Strong fingers pressed the seam of her jeans against her clit, and he pressed his hips tighter against her back, pushing her up against his hand.

Keri shivered, her hands reaching back to grip his thighs and tug him closer. She'd never imagined how erotic being undressed could be. The few lovers she had, had always considered clothes an inconvenience to be dealt with as quickly as possible; preferably with the lights out to avoid any embarrassment on either side.

With Alistair though, it was all so different. Her heart tightened in her chest as she reminded herself again that she had promised to find a way to free him, that what they had was only temporary. Then his mouth was gliding over her skin, and his hands were peeling away her jeans and she left rational thought behind.

His hand was between her legs before her jeans hit the floor, his talented fingers slipping between her already wet folds to stroke and tease. His clothes vanished, and she leaned into him, skin to skin. Keri shuddered, her knees nearly buckling as an orgasm tore through her with the force of a summer storm. His arm wrapped around her, holding her up as she cried out his name, his fingers slick with her arousal.

Before she could catch her breath he had her in his arms, carrying her outside. Alistair looked longingly at the soft grass just beyond the deck, clearly wishing he could reach it. Instead, he lowered her to one of the wrought iron chairs and knelt between her legs, his hands coaxing her to the edge of the seat and spreading her thighs wide.

Keri reached for him, her fingers stroking through his hair, brazenly drawing his head down to where she ached for him to be. His tongue flicked rapidly over her clit, and she cried out sharply at the pleasure of it. He pressed a finger inside, then two, never stopping the assault on her clitoris with his fast moving tongue. His plan was clear to her; he wanted her to come undone, to lose herself until they were both beyond reason, beyond thinking.

Barely able to breathe, Keri let her head fall back, her eyes closing in bliss as her entire world shrank down to the feel of his mouth on her flesh and the fire his touch kindled deep inside her body. Without thinking her hands left his hair, her fingers wrapping around his horns as she sought something to cling to. She felt Alistair shudder, and a wild moan rose up from his chest. He suckled her sweet flesh deep into his mouth, his tongue mercilessly teasing her clitoris as he drove his fingers in and out of her in a rhythm that demanded her surrender.

"Alistair!" She moaned his name and her entire body tensed against the orgasm that was building within her. Half wild with need she bucked her hips against his mouth, her inner walls tightening around his fingers with exquisite pressure. He curved his fingers and sent her senses screaming as his teeth closed gently around her clitoris.

She came hard, barely managing to muffle her screams behind her lips at the last minute as body and mind shattered into crystalline shards of pure bliss. Her world went grey; and it was a long few minutes before she could piece herself back together enough to even lift her head and smile down at a very smug daemon, still kneeling between her thighs.

Without a word he rose up and kissed her tenderly, his arms gathering her close and drawing her down into his lap. She let her legs span his, using her body to guide him back, laying him down beneath her as she answered his kiss with one of her own. Neither of them spoke, using touch and gesture to communicate as she straddled his hips, his thick length trapped beneath. His hands found her breasts, fondling them, letting their weight fall into his palms. She rewarded him with a slow circle of her hips, rubbing herself along his cock. When he growled in pleasure, she lifted herself higher, guiding him to her opening with slow movements until his thick head was pressed just a scant inch inside her.

Feeling wickedly brazen, Keri held herself above him, loving the way his eyes watched her every move. She felt his cock twitch and knew he was waiting for her, letting her control this moment. A wanton smile curved her lips as she sat looked down at him, letting herself slide down his shaft an inch at a time.

Alistair watched raptly, his eyes never leaving the place that they were joined Finally he arched his hips playfully, making her breasts move. "Bounce for me." He grinned up at her.

"Brat!" She exclaimed and then broke into peals of laughter.

His hands moved to her hips, coaxing her to move. "I am, though no one but my mother would ever dare say it aloud before today."

Still laughing, she stuck out her tongue at him and rolled her hips, shuddering as another wave of pleasure flowed through her. Soon she was moving faster, her hands wrapped around his strong wrists to keep her balance.

She rode him like a galloping stallion, his answering thrusts driving him deep inside her as they both raced towards release.

She felt him stiffen, and his eyes met hers, the fire burning in their depths a warning that he was nearing his breaking point. His hands left her hips to capture her breasts in his hands, his fingers rolling and pinching at her nipples.

Feeling his hands on her again sent Keri spinning off into another orgasm, her thighs gripping his hips tightly as she ground herself over him, leaning down to kiss him and scream her pleasure into his mouth. Alistair's hips slammed upward, lifting them both from the deck as he came, his semen pouring into her and she knew that at the same time he took her energy and fed on it until he was sated.

Keri half tumbled into his arms, her limbs rag doll limp and a smile on her face. "That was amazing." She murmured and brushed her lips against his broad chest. He tasted of musk and salt, both their bodies slick with sweat from the summer sun and their recent exertion.

His arms wrapped around her, holding her to him as they lay together in the afterglow, his hands smoothing up and down her bare back. "You're amazing. Watching you orgasm is the most beautiful thing I have ever seen. If I cannot free myself, then promise me I can watch you do that every day, and I will be content with my lot."

She lifted her head and looked into his eyes. "I promise if we can't free you I'll do all I can to make you happy." A surge of sadness filled her, and she fought to hide her feelings before they showed on her face. "But I know we'll find a way, and then you can go home."

He reached up and brushed a strand of hair from her damp cheek, tracing the form of her face with his fingertips. "I hope you're right, I've been gone too long already."

A gentle silence fell between them, both of them lost in their own thoughts. Eventually, Keri moved, separating their bodies with reluctance. "You can't be comfortable lying like this. Why don't we go back inside?"

"Your skin is too fair to be out here much longer, already I can see you've gone pink." He touched her shoulder and nodded in agreement. "And I believe I had plans for us in that shower of yours."

"You're insatiable." She informed him with a squeal of delight as he scooped her back into his arms and carried her into the bathroom.

"Incubi usually are." He grinned down at her. "We have to eat when we can, only those with mates know when we're going to find our next meal."

"Oh lovely, I'm a meal now?"

"A very tasty one." Alistair set her down and swatted her playfully on the rump as he pointed to the shower. "Now, show me how this works, I fear I'm getting hungry again."

"And you complained I was pushy!" She grumbled playfully as she showed him how to adjust the water's temperature and turn the shower on.

"The moment she declared the water hot enough she found herself lifted her into the shower by a pair of powerful hands and seconds later he had followed her in, crowding the space with his six and a half foot frame. She reached past him and found the soap, lathering it in her hands and smoothing it over his shoulders, enjoying the excuse to explore his body.

She worked her way lower, keeping the soap away from him despite several attempts to take it from her. "Uh-uh, it's your turn to be patient," she informed him with a wink and a grin.

Alistair shot her a disgruntled look and relented, surrendering to her ministrations. Soon he was moaning at her touch, clearly enjoying her attentions as she felt his muscles relax beneath her hands. She was enjoying herself too; letting her hands glide all over Alistair's sculpted body. She glanced up at his face, noting the closed eyes and relaxed smile on his handsome face.

She let her hands drift lower, saw the catch in his breathing as her fingers caressed his balls. A wicked thought flashed through her mind, and she acted before she could reconsider, dropping to her knees and wrapping her lips around his semi hard cock, her soap covered hands cupping his scrotum at the same time.

Alistair startled and groaned, his cock hardening instantly. He leaned back against the tiles of the shower stall, his hips already rocking lightly against her mouth. Hot water streamed down their bodies, adding another layer of stimulation to the experience. Enjoying the power she held, Keri got busy, her tongue stroking over every inch of hard flesh.

"Keri." He growled her name as she sucked on him hard, her teeth lightly raking over his sensitive glans. "By Styx woman, don't stop."

Her response was a low laugh she knew would vibrate through him, and she was pleased to note it made his thighs quake in response. He gripped the soap dish with one hand, the other reaching down to rest on her head, shielding her face from the continuous cascade of water. Over and over her tongue measured his length, only pausing to flick rapid-fire over the tip of his penis, lapping at it until he groaned in pleasure.

As he groaned a warning Keri bowed her head, opened her mouth wide and swallowed him deep, so deep her throat muscles stroked him as she swallowed again and again. She felt him tense and then she was swallowing down his seed, the sharp crack of something breaking nearly drowned out by his roars of pleasure.

Keri was back in his arms before he opened his eyes again, kissing him and laughing as she pried the handle of the soap dish out of his fingers.

"You broke my shower." She informed him, holding up the broken fixture.

"You broke me first." He answered her gruffly and lifted her off the floor to kiss her, turning them both so that his back was shielding her from the water. She wrapped her legs around his hips as he backed her into the tiled wall and held her there, his kisses deep and demanding.

Keri's moaned, and the broken handle fell to the bathmat, forgotten as her need for him swept everything else away. His thick cock pressed against her slit, and she moaned, gripping him tighter as he rocked his hips and breached her channel by the barest inch before stopping, poised just on the verge of pleasuring them both.

"Again? Already?" She wriggled her body, gaining a scant quarter inch of him inside her.

"Again, already. I'm becoming addicted to you Keri, I can't get enough." With that he drove himself in deep, sinking into her wet heat with a low groan.

Keri buried her face into his neck, clinging to him as he took her hard, the wet slap of skin on skin filling the small space. Every nerve ending tingled and flared as he filled her, stretched her body around his. She whimpered in need, closed her teeth on his skin as the pleasure bordered on the edge of pain.

Harder, faster his body claimed hers with an almost brutal intensity, teeth nipping at each other's skin, marking each other in their pleasure. They came together, two voices crying out in ecstasy and then she'd gone limp in his arms, her head resting against the powerful curve of his shoulder.

"Keri?" Alistair shook her gently; his voice was thick with worry when she didn't answer him.

With a soft curse, he'd gathered her back into his arms and stepped out of the shower. "Keri? Answer me Beautiful."

She felt like she was floating, and it took an act of will just to lift her head and open her eyes. "Hi."

"I hurt you didn't I?" Regret filled his voice as turned off the shower and reached for a towel, draping it over her awkwardly since she was still in his arms. "I'm so sorry."

"Hurt? No." Keri's noticed her hands were trembling as she took the towel and dried her face. "I think—" She blushed slightly and tried again to explain. "I think that was so good I passed out for a moment."

Relief replaced the frown on Alistair's face and then his lips twitched into the beginnings of a smug smile. "I made you pass out? Really?"

"Yes, you did. I'm never going to hear the end of this now am I?" She reached up to smooth the last of his frown away with her fingertips. "You didn't hurt me at all. I don't believe you would ever hurt me."

Alistair set her on her feet carefully and grabbed another towel, drying her off as he spoke. "I would never hurt you intentionally, but you make me more than a little crazy. When I'm with you I forget myself, forget you are a mortal and far more fragile than I am."

"Hey." She reached out and lifted his chin so he was looking at her. "When you forgot yourself a moment ago, it was the most incredible feeling I've ever had. Being with you is always amazing, but that was something else again. Maybe mortals are tougher than you think, or maybe you're not nearly as big and bad as you imagine yourself to be, but either way, I don't want you to treat me like I'm made of glass. If you hurt me, I'll tell you."

She stood on tiptoe and kissed the corner of his mouth before whispering, "But I'm glad you care."

* * * *

All the air left Alistair's lungs as the impact of her words hit him like a physical blow. He did care. He'd shared the beds of thousands of women, but he'd never really cared about any of them. Not until Keri. A warning sounded in his head, conveyed in the voice one of his oldest mentors.

She's mortal, you can't stay with her. She'll grow old, and you'll have to find other women to feed off of. It never works, you know that. It only ever brings pain and heartache.

He took a half step back and lifted his head, moving out of her reach. Until they knew for certain he could not be freed, he wouldn't let himself fall for her, or her for him. They had to keep this simple, or he'd break every promise he'd made not to hurt her.

She came down off her toes and moved away from him, her normally expressive face carefully blank. With a casualness he knew was hiding her hurt at his reaction, she asked, "Why don't I go make us something to eat? I don't know about you, but I'm starving."

Alistair followed her out, having conjured a pair of modern jeans and a black t-shirt for himself. "Food sounds good, thanks."

"That is a very neat trick." She flashed him a smile that seemed stilted and stiff and got dressed, her body language completely closed off. "Nice clothing by the way, if it weren't for the horns nobody would ever suspect you're not human."

Damn it, he'd hurt her already. Regret flared in his heart, but it didn't deter him. Alistair looked into her eyes and tried to make the warning clear. "Horns or no, we both know I'm not a mortal man." He turned and flipped on her laptop. "I'll be doing some research while you're in the kitchen. Maybe somewhere in this Internet thing is the way to get me free."

She stopped in the doorway and looked back to where he was seated. "If there's a way, we'll find it. I know how much you want to be free." Then she was gone, leaving Alistair alone with his research and his regrets. The last thing in the world he wanted to do was hurt Keri, but she was mortal, he was a daemon, and he knew that if he wasn't careful, things between them were going to get very complicated, fast.

CHAPTER SEVEN

That night the dream came again. She was back on the same beach, running through the storm. This time, the sense of loss was even more painful than before, though she still didn't know what it was she had lost. The wind threw up sea spray that lashed at her skin like icy whips, and she cried out in fear, but the wind stole her voice away, and her cries went unheard. A distant roar filled her ears, and Keri cringed, knowing what would come next. She stopped running and turned around to face the massive wave that was hurtling towards her, a wall of dark water she had no way to escape. As the chill water slammed down on her, she screamed and woke up bolt upright with a choking wail of terror on her lips.

She felt strong arms wrap around her, tugging her against the warm and comforting bulk of Alistair's body. She could hear his heart pounding against her cheek and realized it raced nearly as fast as hers. She clung to him, her terror fading slowly as his soft words soothed her fears. He may have pulled away from her earlier, but he was here now, and she needed him.

"It's alright Keri, I'm here, it was only a dream."

Damn, do I hate these nightmares. The thought rose up out of her shattered wits as Keri came back to her senses. "Did I wake you up? I'm sorry."

"I couldn't sleep; I was reading out on the deck." He lifted her into his lap and cradled her next to his chest. "I should have been here."

"It wouldn't have made any difference; the dreams come no matter who's with me." Keri sighed and wrapped her arms around his neck, needing to feel his solid strength around her. "I once lashed out in a dream and gave my husband a black eye. He hated sleeping with me when I had these weird dream spells." She struggled to keep the shame and embarrassment from her voice and failed. "He started sleeping in another bedroom; he said it was so he could get good night's sleep. I suppose that's when everything really started to fall apart. I drove him out of our bed."

"He sounds like a very weak, selfish sort of man. A true mate would have stayed with you and tried to determine why you keep having these dreams." Alistair threaded his hands through her hair, letting it fall through his fingers. "Was the dream the same one you were having when I first came to you?"

"That's the one. Beach, storm, screaming, big wave, crunch, and then I'm awake again." She drew a ragged breath. "I hate it."

"How long have you had it? Since you were a child?" He asked, his voice still low and soothing.

"This dream? This one started a few months ago. At first it wasn't often, but lately, I've had it nearly every night."

"You didn't have it last night," He pointed out.

"No, you're right, I didn't. I had it that afternoon, but you came and changed the dream, and I didn't have it again until tonight."

Alistair was quiet for a long moment. "When you have these dreams, do they ever come to pass?"

"What?" Keri felt a wave of dread wash over her. *How did he know?*

"These dreams, the ones that repeat themselves, do they ever come true?" His hand cupped her cheek, stroking it gently with his thumb.

Tears welled up in Keri's eyes, and she jerked away from his touch. "I don't want to talk about it." She was suddenly lost in a flood of memories; her begging her Dad not to go away for the weekend, being too young to make him understand she'd seen him die in her nightmares. It was easier to not remember at all than to have to live with the memory of her failure to save him. Every dark, painful moment of her life she'd seen in her dreams before they happened, and she'd never been able to change a single outcome.

"I'll take that as a yes." His hand dropped to her shoulder, and he drew her close, his hands soothing her as she trembled against him. "It's alright Keri, we won't talk about it anymore if you don't want to."

"I don't want to." Her words came out sharper than she'd intended and Keri winced inwardly. She was always messing things up between them. She cast about for something to fill the growing silence.

"Would you mind if I left the house for a while tomorrow? I need to run into town and buy groceries, and I thought I'd pay my neighbor a visit. She was kind enough to give me some fresh eggs the other day, and I baked her desert in thanks. I'd like to give it to her, but I don't want to leave you alone if you aren't okay with it."

"You can't stay with me every minute of the day, that would make you as much a prisoner as I am." His tone was joking, but she thought she heard a trace of wistfulness beneath the surface.

Keri smiled and fought to tamp down the hope that flared at his faint show of disappointment. "Then I'll do that tomorrow and leave you to your research. I meant to ask, have you found anything helpful?"

"Maybe." He drew her down and snuggled her close before drawing the covers over them, spooning his body around hers. "It's likely nothing, but I've found two mentions of the same item, and it's more than I had to go on before."

"An item? What item? Do we need to find one to free you?"

"It's a small medallion, it would be forged in the same metal that's inlaid into this bed." In all the years I have been a prisoner I have never seen it, but if I understand the references, there may be one hidden somewhere in the bed itself. If it exists, it's what holds me here." His voice was a low rumble near her ear. "When you restored the bed and assembled it, did you see something like that?"

"A medallion about the size of a toonie, made of silvery metal?" Keri's heart slammed in her chest and then shattered into pieces as she recalled the metal disc set into the top of one column. When she told him about it, he'd leave her, and she wasn't ready for him to walk out of her life. She'd be alone again, and deep in her broken heart she knew she'd never find another man who would ever compare to the one she was about to lose. Her mouth formed the lie before she even knew what she would say. "No, I don't remember anything like that. I'm sorry Alistair."

"I will keep researching. It was unlikely the key to my freedom would be so easy to find. So tell me, what is a toonie?"

"A two dollar coin, about an inch wide." She explained, trying to stay calm as screams of panic at what she had just done threatened to drown out every other thought in her head. "The one dollar coin ended up with the nickname of a "loonie" for the loon stamped on one side, so when they came up with a two dollar coin, it got called the toonie."

"A strange name for a coin. But you humans are a strange race."

"Don't insult the human who is going to feed you all your favorite things tomorrow." She scolded him lightly. "At least, I will if you tell me what they are. We'll both work in the morning and spend the rest of the day enjoying ourselves. How does that sound?" She mentally added, *and then the next morning I'll tell you about the medallion, and you'll leave me.*

"That sounds perfect." He murmured and brushed a kiss to her shoulder before slipping out of their bed. "I'll just bring the laptop inside and be right back."

She watched him walk away, the moonlight bright enough she could see every breathtaking detail of his body. She had to bite her lip sharply to stop the tears that threatened to spill down her cheeks. Losing him was going to hurt, but to keep him she had to keep him prisoner, and she couldn't do that to him.

He returned to their bed and curled up beside her once more, his arm curving around her waist to hold her close. "Now go to sleep. I'll be right here, guarding your dreams."

Even though she was tired, it took Keri a long time to fall asleep. Her thoughts were full of recriminations at the lie she had told, and everything was tinged with sadness at knowing it was all coming to an end. Her lie had bought her one more day, and she'd make it as perfect as she could. One shining memory to hold onto when she faced the emptiness she knew was coming.

Long after her breathing had deepened and she had drifted back into sleep, Alistair lay awake. Keri affected him in ways no woman ever had, and much as he would like to pretend otherwise, it was more than simply because he had been alone for so long. He watched her sleeping beside him, fascinated by the freckles that dusted the pale skin of her shoulders. His promises to her, to himself, everything that had seemed to clear just a few hours ago, he knew now it wasn't going to be that simple. He wanted her, yes, but it was more than that.

His fingers brushed through her long red curls, pausing to touch the love bite on her neck. He had marked her once, and by Styx he wanted to mark her again, in a way that would tell everyone she was his and only his.

Alistair shook his head, amazed at the thoughts he was having. He needed to free himself soon and go home. If anyone knew a way for him to keep his beautiful Keri, it was the Elders. But until he freed himself from this cursed spell and returned home, he could not offer her anything permanent, it wouldn't be fair. He'd have to keep his hopes to himself.

CHAPTER EIGHT

Keri woke with a shuddering moan as Alistair's mouth sampled her breast, his golden brown eyes gleaming with mischief as he watched her wake up. His fingers were already resting on her mound, brushing against her labia with feather light touches. Within seconds she was awake, desire tightening her nipples to hard nubs and a pool of molten need gathering between her legs.

"Good morning." She mewled and arched beneath him, stretching her body out in an invitation to continue.

He flicked his tongue over her nipple again and then lifted his head to smile at her. "Good morning Beautiful. I tried to let you sleep in, but I couldn't wait any longer to have you."

He leaned over to lave her other breast as his fingers pressed a fraction of an inch deeper into her folds, teasing her. She bucked her hips against his fingers and gasped as his fingers slid deep and then deeper as he entered her with two fingers, his thumb unerringly finding her clitoris and pressing down firmly.

He worked her clit mercilessly, his fingers curling inside, finding the sensitive spot on her vaginal wall and caressing her there.

He seemed determined to make her come hard, his touch seeking out every hotspot she had. "Come for me Beautiful." He murmured.

Keri moaned and writhed on the bed, her breath coming in short pants as she squirmed against the relentless pleasure of his fingers. She saw him watching her intently as her hands burrowed into the sheets, kneading them with frantic strength as her orgasm began to build.

"Come for me, show me how good it feels," he commanded her, increasing the speed of his fingers as they thrust in and out of her. "I want to taste your pleasure, Keri."

"So good!" Keri cried out. Her inner muscles clamped around him, and she arched her hips up hard, her movements wild as her body reacted with raw instinct to the pleasure he was lavishing on her. She gasped brokenly and shuddered, trying to catch her breath. He never gave her that chance. Instead, he moved quickly to pull her legs over the edge of the bed and flipped her over so she was face down, the sheets she had clung to now tangled around her hands.

"That was good, but I want more." He half growled as his hands found her thighs, parted and lifted them until she was angled perfectly. He moved closer and pulled her to him, thrusting into her without warning and she could feel her body stretch to take him. "You feel like you were made for me!" He groaned as their bodies met with no space left between them.

She was so full of him it was almost painful, and she bit back a full-throated moan as she wriggled against him, asking him for even more. She gripped him with her innermost muscles and released, then did it again; she teased and begged with each flex of her body, needing him to take her, needing him to move.

"Say it Keri." His voice was a rough growl. "Tell me what you want."

"You, I want you. Please Alistair, I need you."

He took her then, hard and fast. His hips driving hard, the delicious friction between them building to a blazing fire of need.

Keri cried out his name, again and again, encouraging him, begging him as she clung to the bed. The pleasure mounted until at last her world shattered into bliss, her hips thrusting wildly and her body shuddering hard. She came, and he kept going, her cries muffled by the mattress as he deliberately pushed her past her limits.

He felt her come, her energy punching through him, nearly bringing him to his knees. The clench of her around his cock, the flood of wetness had brought him to the edge of his control, but he wanted more. He wanted to lay claim to her, body and soul.

She moaned again, turning her head towards the mirror. "Alistair, look." She inclined her head towards the mirror, clearly enthralled by the image of the two of them together. He glanced up, following her gaze and groaned as he took in the vision of her beneath him, his body driving into hers over and over. It was his undoing, knowing she saw what he did; the image of the two of them entwined and caught in the thrall of passion. He came in a torrent, feeling as though he were turned inside out and drained dry. Her release was nearly as wild as his, their voices both filling the room as they cried out together.

Alistair withdrew and lowered her legs carefully back to the bed, feeling her muscles tremble beneath his hands. He lifted her, moving her closer to the middle so he could crawl in beside her, still trying to catch his breath. She snuggled into him, laying her head on his chest, one arm draped over his stomach as she tried to speak.

"Wow," was all she managed to say the first time. She cleared her throat and tried again. "That was...I don't think there is a word for what that was."

"Magic," he said. "That was magic."

Keri laughed and hugged him. "Everything about you is magic."

He lifted his head and pressed a feather-light kiss to her brow, tasting the salty sweet tang of her sweat on his lips. "This kind of magic takes two."

They stayed in bed a while longer, wrapped around each other in a comfortable silence neither of them wanted to break. Finally, Keri sighed and sat up, regret in her eyes as she left his side.

"I have to get showered and bring that crumble to Samantha. After that, I'll hit town, and I'll be back before lunch." She walked to the bathroom without bothering to pull on a robe, leaving him to enjoy the view of her delectable body for a few moments more. "I'll bring in breakfast for you before I go."

"Thank you." He paused as if about to say something more, but then he lay back and closed his eyes again, leaving her to start her morning. *Don't ask her to stay that isn't fair to her.* He reminded himself as she left him alone.

* * * *

An hour later she was walking up the long driveway that led to her neighbor's house, laughing as her arrival was heralded by a number of chickens that ran ahead of her clucking loudly. By the time she neared the front door Samantha was already standing in it, waving her inside.

"Coffee?" She offered as she gestured for Keri to take a seat in her cozy kitchen. "Oh, you baked! Marvelous. My son is coming over for the holiday, and he loves fresh baked anything."

"Holiday?" Keri was confused for a moment and then realized what day it was. "I totally forgot, its July first, Canada Day! I've been so busy getting things settled I totally lost track of the days."

Samantha handed her a cup of coffee and grinned. "Moving can do that to you. By the time I got my husband, and I packed up and moved out here, I didn't know if I was coming or going for a month!"

"If I have my way we'll not be moving again, too many headaches. My son, Trevor, is a gypsy, never in one place very long. I don't know how he does it."

She slanted Keri a sidelong look. "I'd try to set you up with him, but I know better than to even try. He never sticks around long enough for a girl to gaff him. Heaven knows I've tried."

Keri blushed and shook her head. "Even if he were looking to be gaffed, I'm involved. Well, I am, I think. I may not be for long, though. It's complicated."

"Oh Honey, when it comes to men? It's always complicated."

"You can say that again." Keri agreed and toasted Samantha with her coffee mug. "I met someone, and everything happened so fast, I'm not sure how we got here. But we're so different; his life is never going to be like mine."

"Different isn't always a bad thing. My husband is an accountant. When I met him, he was as buttoned up and stuffy as they come. I never looked twice; he wasn't anything I thought I could possibly want. I'm a painter who talks to her chickens and never fit in with the regular folks. Different as night and day we were, so I completely forgot about him. He didn't forget about me, though, and when I finally gave in and got to know him, I discovered we complimented each other. He keeps me grounded, and I stop him from closing himself off from the world. I can't imagine my life without him in it."

Keri sighed. "It's more than just that. Alistair's looking for something here, and when he finds it, he'll be going home."

"So you're serious, and he's not?"

"I don't know what we are, not really. It's only been a couple of days."

Samantha burst out laughing. "A whirlwind courtship? No wonder you lost track of time. Those will send your whole world out of whack.

I know you didn't come her looking for advice, but you're going to get some anyway. Don't hang on too tight, just enjoy the ride. If fate has plans for the two of you, then he'll be back. You can't force love, and the more you try, the faster it slips through your fingers."

"This was so much easier when I'd sworn off men, dating, and risk," Keri muttered into her coffee.

"Easier sure, but where's the fun in that?" Samantha asked. "To quote one of my favorite singers, "Life is not tried, it is merely survived if you're standing outside the fire."

"Fire burns," Keri observed softly as she took another sip of her coffee.

"And burns heal." Samantha leaned forward and took Keri's hand, turning it so it was palm up, her fingers running lightly along the lines of her hand. "You've had so much heartache, Honey, I can see it." She traced over a deep line that cut across Keri's palm. "But you have to let it go. See here? Two paths diverging down your life line. You've got choices to make, don't be afraid to make the right one. Depending on what you choose, your life could go in very different directions, but once you make your choice, there's no going back.

Keri stared at Samantha, unsure what had just happened. "What?"

Samantha shook her head as if clearing it and smiled ruefully. "I apologize, I should have asked before reading your palm that way, but something compelled me to do it." Samantha let go of Keri's hand, and she downed the rest of her coffee. "You've got a fair share of the sight yourself, why don't you use it?"

"Me? No." Keri shook her head and set down her mug so hard it clattered on the table top.

"Yes, you do. But you're frightened of it. No one ever taught you how to use it, did they?" Samantha's voice was softer now. "If ever you want to learn, I'd be happy to teach you. It's nothing to be afraid of, it's a gift. But for now, just remember what I told you. Change is coming, and you've got choices to make. Be brave, and when the time comes, listen to your heart."

A car door slammed shut outside, followed by another one. "My boys are back. Do you want to stay a bit longer?"

"No, I should go and leave you to catch up with your son." Keri stood and on impulse came over and hugged Samantha. "Thank you for the coffee and everything."

The front door opened, and a male voice called out "Mom? Where's my hug?"

"I'm in the kitchen!" Samantha's face lit up as she heard her son's voice.

Seconds later a fast-moving blur of muscle and sun bleached blonde hair passed through the kitchen and lifted Samantha into a bear hug. "Nice to see you Mom, what smells good? Did you bake?"

"Put me down, we have company!" The smaller woman swatted her son on the shoulder and laughed before pointing to Keri. "Trevor, this is Keri, Tammy's granddaughter. She's just moved back to the island. And that's her baking you smell, not mine."

"Oops." Trevor set his mother down and grinned at Keri, his playful expression upping her first assessment of him from handsome to "drop dead gorgeous." He was tall and well-muscled judging from the way he filled out his shirt, and his grey-blue eyes were just like his mother's, kind and full of laughter. "I didn't realize we had company. Nice to meet you." He held out his hand in greeting.

Keri took his hand and shook it, waiting for her tongue to tie itself into its usual knots when faced with a handsome face, but nothing happened. Instead, she returned his smile and replied without a single stammer.

"Hi. You're mom was nice enough to give me some eggs the other day so I just popped by to deliver a thank you. I hope you like raspberries."

"I am a fan of all things berry, but most especially raspberries." He let go of her hand and turned to grin at Samantha. "Good thinking, finding a neighbor who bakes. I'd come home more often if you didn't use the smoke detector as a timer." He ducked a playful swat from his mother and bounced back a few feet, out of reach.

"Behave yourself!" Samantha chided and rolled her eyes. "This is what happens when he is out of my influence for too long. He gets full of sass and forgets I can still turn him over my knee."

Keri burst out laughing. "On that note, I will leave you to your reunion, Happy Canada Day!" She passed Tom on the way out and gave him a wave. "I'm Keri, your neighbor. I dropped off some baking with Samantha. If you hurry Trevor may not have eaten it all just yet."

He waved back and broke into a jog, clearly headed for the kitchen.

As Keri slipped behind the wheel of her car she wondered at the easy way she'd handled Trevor. Normally a man like that would have her tripping over herself with nerves, but that hadn't happened. *Alistair.* His name popped into her head. *You don't care about other guys anymore because you have the one you want.*

Her fingers tightened on the steering wheel, and she mused out loud. "But I don't have him, not for long." She felt tears welling up in her eyes, and she bit her lip, clamping down on her emotions and putting them aside as a tiny voice whispered in her mind. *Everyone leaves. Brent, Gran, my parents; nobody ever stays. Alistair isn't going to be any different.*

She took a deep breath and cleared her mind, gathering up all the thoughts that raced through her head and then locking them all away. She'd face all that tomorrow.

Today she was going to do what Samantha had advised. She was going to enjoy the ride.

It took her longer than she planned to get the shopping done. Ganges was stuffed full of locals and tourists, all enjoying the festivities. A classic car show had taken over the park, and everywhere people were clad in red and white outfits while kids proudly sported faces painted up with maple leafs and small Canadian flags. She'd managed to find nearly everything she'd wanted, and when she reached home, it took two trips to get it all inside. Alistair was standing in the hallway to greet her, frustration evident on his face as he pressed against the magical barrier that prevented him coming to the kitchen.

"I'll be right there." She called out as she tossed the ice cream into the freezer before it melted. The rest could wait, but the Haagen-Dazs was already looking decidedly mushy. She'd abandoned her original plan of cooking up a feast, realizing she didn't want to spend her last day with Alistair cooped up in the kitchen. Instead, she'd found a bake-at-home pizza with the works, and several bags worth of junk food, treats, and frozen appetizers. Whatever they didn't eat today, Keri could use as therapy tomorrow after he was gone. "No more of that." She scolded herself out loud and went to find Alistair.

He was still standing in the hall, leaning up against the wall, waiting. "No more of what?" He asked just before dropping a sizzling kiss to her lips.

Keri ignored his question and happily kissed him back instead, her lips parting as her tongue twined with his. By the time the kiss ended neither of them could remember that he'd asked her anything at all.

"Hi, miss me?" She grinned up at him.

"I did. Did you accomplish everything you set out to do? Or do you need to go again?"

Her stomach did a little flip-flop as he looked down at her hopefully.

"I'm not going anywhere; I'm all yours for the rest of the day. I forgot today was a national holiday, so the town was very busy. That's why it took so long."

"A festival?" He asked, a smile curving his lips as she told him she was all his.

"A big one, and it means that if we head up to the roof tonight, we can see the fireworks down in the harbor. You game for a little reckless roof climbing in the name of pretty lights?"

"Is it dangerous for you? Will I be able to get there without hitting the end of my leash?" A look of pure frustration crossed his face as he gestured to the bed.

"Dangerous? No, not really, we just need to be careful. My family has been doing it for years. There's a spot where the roof barely slopes, it's perfect. I'm pretty sure we can manage to do it without you reaching the five pace limit. At least as long as it works vertically as well as horizontal." Keri stood on tiptoe and kissed him. "We'll figure it out."

CHAPTER NINE

When twilight came, they were ensconced on a blanket up on the roof, watching as the purple and gold sunset faded into a star filled night. Keri's fingers were entwined with his, and she was curled into his side, her eyes on sky as they waited for the firework display to start.

Their day had been perfect, a picnic on the deck, then an afternoon of lovemaking that had lasted for hours. It had been idyllic, coming together and then dozing off in each other's arms, only to wake and begin the whole cycle anew. Keri had drawn them both a bath and added far too much bubble stuff to it, producing a tub of hot water and foam that enveloped them both once they both got in, towering almost to their chins and leaving the bathroom floor awash while they both laughed and made love again, adding another wash of water to the already sopping floor.

A night breeze blew up from the harbor, bringing with it the sounds of the crowd and the scent of grilling meat. He felt Keri shiver, and she snuggled closer to him for warmth. "I should have remembered to bring us jackets."

"I think I can fix that."

He winked at her and then concentrated for a moment, and as Keri watched with fascination, his modern clothing shimmered like a heat mirage and transformed into one of his favorite outfits. His legs were clad in dark trousers and soft leather boots that rose to his knee. His shirt was now long sleeved and loose, the ties to fasten it shut left unlaced to mid chest. He lifted a portion of the cloak he now wore over her shoulders and drew her closer, wrapping it around them both like a blanket.

"I am never going to get used to that." She murmured and stroked her fingers over the heavy fabric.

"It comes in handy, especially when the weather changes suddenly." He drew her head to his shoulder, resting his chin lightly on the crown of her hair as they stared out at the night.

Alistair knew he'd never been this happy, not in his adult life. Being with Keri had given him more than renewed strength; she had renewed his spirit too. He'd been so close to letting go and fading away, but not anymore. He'd realized how much she had changed his life when she had gone out, and even in those brief hours he'd missed her presence. If he couldn't go for less than a day without her, there was no way he could fool himself into believing he could leave her behind if ever he got free. Somehow, he'd find a way to make it work. He wouldn't accept any other option; Keri was his.

"Keri, I wanted to tell you..." That's all he managed to say before the first fireworks bloomed in the sky and Keri squealed in delight.

The sky had filled with fountains of flame and starbursts of sparkling color, the snap and pop of every explosion rolling through the air and making it impossible to speak. The display lasted for ages; every new volley more spectacular than the last until the entire town was lit by a canopy of multicolored fire that filled the night with light and noise. As the grand finale finished the roar of the crowd could be heard, cheers and clapping that rivaled the fireworks for pure noise.

"Did you like it?" She asked him.

"I've never seen the like. It was beautiful and very loud. When will they do that again?"

"It's a once a year event I'm afraid. Though there will be a smaller display in the autumn, for Halloween. It's not even close to this scale, though."

"I suppose it would not be nearly so amazing if it happened too often." He lowered his head to hers, unable to resist the urge to kiss her. His fingers wrapped into her hair forgot everything but the sweet tasting woman he held in his arms. It was the wind that finally broke their kiss, the cool night air drawing another shiver from Keri that Alistair knew had nothing to do with their kiss.

"Let's go back inside before you get too cold." He'd stood carefully and then offered Keri his hand, helping her up beside him.

"Good idea. We'll get back inside and then I'll go grab us some ice cream, a perfect way to end this evening."

"Who says this is the end of anything?" He asked and scooped up the blanket, tossing it off the roof and then wrapped his arms around her. "I've decided it's not safe for you to climb down alone. If you fell and hurt yourself, I would be useless to you. I cannot protect you the way you should be protected and cared for. Not until I am free."

"You take better care of me than any man I have ever known." She argued back.

He crouched down and lifted her into his arms. "Hold onto me. I am getting us down a safer way."

She did as he instructed, wrapping her arms tightly around his neck and burying her face in the curve of his shoulder as he stepped to the edge of the roof.

"You're not going to—."

He jumped, landing easily in the grassy yard. "There, safe and sound."

"Are you crazy?" She demanded as she stared up at the roof they'd just left. "That wasn't safe!"

He grinned, amused at her outburst and enjoying the way she felt in his arms. He stopped her protests with a kiss before lowering her to the ground to stand on her own. "Of course, it was. Being with you has made me more powerful than I have ever been. Our powers develop over time, as we age they grow stronger. I've been locked away without the energy I needed to use them until you found me. I've been getting stronger from the first time we met in your dreams. That small leap was nothing for me, Beauty. Don't worry; I wouldn't risk you getting hurt."

* * * *

Keri didn't want to hear about getting hurt, not when their time was coming to an end. Pain and heartbreak were on tomorrow's agenda, and she wasn't ready to face them just yet. They still had tonight, and she intended to make the most of it.

"Ice cream, I need ice cream." She declared and headed into the house, knowing he'd need to go more slowly, edging around the wall of the house because of the limits of his prison.

She was hunting for the ice cream scoop when she'd heard her phone buzzing. She'd nearly forgotten it existed, having never checked it since Alistair had appeared in her life. Grinning at herself for forgetting, she recalled Samantha's words about whirlwind courtships and things getting out of whack as she dug the cell out of her purse and checked her voicemail.

The first call was time stamped from yesterday afternoon. "Hi Ms. Anderson, this is Josh, from the antique store. I am very embarrassed by all this, but it seems that my clerk gave your name to a woman who was also interested in the bed. I wasn't aware she'd called inquiring about it a few days before you came in. Now the sale was final, and there's no problem at all, but she somehow managed to charm my staff into giving her your name and information. I just wanted to apologize for this; it's against company policy to give out a customer's information. I'm not sure how it happened, and if there's anything I can do to make it up to you, please just let me know."

Keri shrugged. Maybe she'd sell the bed to this other woman. Once Alistair was gone, she couldn't bear the thought of sleeping in it again. Not after everything that had happened. She hit a button and called up the second message, time stamped only a few hours ago. A woman's voice, smooth and charming filled her ear. "Hello there. I hope you're having a lovely holiday Ms. Anderson. My name is Cora, and I believe you've purchased something I am interested in buying; an heirloom bed that once belonged to my family. I have been tracking it down for quite some time, and I was hoping you'd consider selling it to me. It's got great sentimental value. I'll be out to the island tomorrow to talk to you about it in person, I've reserved a spot on the first ferry, I hope you don't mind. I'll see you then."

Keri stood in the kitchen, the ice cream forgotten as she stared at her phone. "Oh shit!" She swore and tried to fight back the sick twist of panic that filled her gut. She turned and ran back to the bedroom, frantically calling Alistair's name.

"What's wrong? What is it?" He met her at the doorway, worry clearly etched on his handsome face.

"You need to hear this." She punched up the message and handed the phone to him with shaking hands, showing him how to hold it to his ear. She hugged her arms to herself and tried to calm down. Tried to tell herself it couldn't possibly be *that* Cora, it was impossible. One look at Alistair's face as he heard the voice recording was enough to tell her otherwise.

Impossible or not, it was her. As Keri watched in misery all the color drained out of Alistair's face and his eyes blazed with a golden light that had no warmth to it. When the message was done, he hurled the phone across the room, shattering it. Then he threw back his head and roared.

Keri took several steps back, suddenly afraid of him. For the first time, her heart recognized what he truly was; not a man but a daemon, dangerous and powerful beyond her understanding.

He reached out to her, his jaw tight but his eyes full of regret as she moved away from him. "Keri, no, please. Don't fear me."

"I'm trying not to, but it's hard." Her pulse pounded in her ears, and she reminded herself that he had sworn to never hurt her. "It's her, isn't it?" She asked softly as one hand lifted and took his outstretched hand. "She found you, and she is coming to take you back."

Strong fingers wrapped around her hand and tugged her into his arms, crushing her to him in a hold that left her barely able to breathe. "Aye, it's her. I won't let anything happen to you Keri, I swear it. I'll die before I let her touch you. I'll find a way to end it, there will be nothing left for her to find, just you and an empty piece of furniture. She won't hurt you if you don't tell her what happened; she'll think I died long before you found the bed."

"No." Keri nearly choked on the word, tears already burning her eyes. "No!" She said it again, louder. "You're not going to die Alistair. You don't have to. She's never going to be able to use you again."

"There's no time." He buried his face in her hair, every word he spoke heavy with rage and grief. "If we'd had more time, maybe we'd have found a way."

She pulled out of his hug and literally climbed his body until she was within reach of his mouth, kissing him with every ounce of her being, her entire body wrapped around him. He kissed her back, his lips branding hers as he lifted her higher and held her as though he'd never let her go.

Time lost all meaning, and they lost themselves in each other, clinging to the last bit of comfort they could take from the other.

It was Alistair who finally lifted his head, staring down at her with grim resolution in his eyes. "I have to go now, my beautiful Keri. What I need to do, it will take time."

"No, it won't." She cupped his cheek tenderly and drew a shaky breath. "Take me to the bed."

"There's no time—" He argued, but she laid a trembling finger over his lips.

"Trust me, please." She felt his muscles bunch as he lifted her higher into his arms and carried her to the bed. "Boost me to your shoulders, I need to be higher."

He did so in silence, not yet understanding what she was doing. She managed to get herself perched on his shoulders and pointed to one of the columns.

"That one, I need to get closer." He walked over to it and put a hand against the post to steady them both while she reached up and tried to dig the medallion out with her nails. She struggled for purchase against the polished metal, the edge nearly flush with the wood.

"What are you doing Keri?" Alistair's voice was low and cooler than she'd ever heard it. He stared up at her, doubt and distrust showing clearly as the first inklings of understanding dawned.

"Saving you from her." She answered with a whimper of pain as she felt a fingernail tear. "Damn it, why won't this thing release?" A flare of blue-green light surrounded her hand, and they both heard a distinctive *snick* come from the top of the column. Keri held her breath and tried again to lift it out, and this time, the medallion lifted easily into her hand.

"Put me down." She directed him, her eyes fixed on the piece of metal in her hand, a trace of her blood smeared over the disturbing image etched into the face. As he lowered her to the ground, she heard him growl in disbelief as he saw what she was holding.

"You lied to me." The accusation was as raw as his voice.

"I'm sorry." She stammered and offered the medallion up to him with shaking hands. "I just—I wanted—please Alistair... I didn't mean to—"

"You LIED!" He bellowed at her, his expression one of pure pain as he stared at her, then at the medallion. He took it from her with shaking hands and stepped backward, putting distance between them. "I was willing to do anything for you Keri, I would have died to protect you, and you lied to me!"

She opened her mouth to protest, to try and explain it was only for this one day. Before she could utter a word he was gone, vanishing so quickly it made her head spin. The last thing she saw was his beautiful eyes, full of hurt and rage as he disappeared out of her life as suddenly as he had come into it.

"Alistair!" She sobbed his name and reached out to where he'd been standing only a second before. The world tilted at an odd angle and Keri found herself on the floor, her arms curled around herself as she cried. She stayed there a long time until her muscles stiffened and the cold seeped into her joints.

Finally, she got to her feet and wandered to the bathroom in a daze, splashing water on her tear-swollen face. "He's free." She told her reflection in a voice rough and raw from crying. "He may hate you, but at least he's free."

Keri felt like she was thinking through a thick wrapping of cotton, every thought seemed dull and fuzzy. She made her way to the kitchen and spied the ice cream melting on the counter.

She put it back in the freezer and then kept tidying; dishes, counters, she even scrubbed the floor, anything to keep busy and distract her from the pain.

It was well past midnight when she was done, the entire kitchen spotless and gleaming. She headed back to her bedroom and started stripping the bed, everything going into a pile on the floor. His scent lingered on the fabric, and she fought back another wave of tears as she gathered it all up and headed to the washing machine. He may be gone, but by the time Cora arrived she needed to get rid of every trace of evidence that Alistair had ever been there at all.

It had taken most of the night, but she'd done it. Even the browsing history of her laptop had been deleted by the time she let herself fall into an exhausted doze on the couch just as dawn came. Not that she got any real rest. Her dreams were fragmented, full of darkness and grief and when she woke only a few short hours later, she felt as if she hadn't slept at all. Knowing that her guest would be arriving soon, she turned on the coffee maker and went to shower. She had a role to play, and it was going to take a full tank of hot water, a big pot of coffee and a whole heap of luck to ensure Cora believed that Alistair had escaped long ago, and the bed was only a bed.

* * * *

Alistair was ablaze with rage, letting it wash over and consume him. Hot fury was so much easier to accept than the empty place in his heart Keri's betrayal had caused. Keri, who had ensorcelled him and then betrayed his trust and his heart. He crossed through the veil and let himself be guided home, trying to forget the haunted look in Keri's tear filled eyes as he vanished. He stepped through the gateway and bent his thoughts to ones of home, knowing that both portal and residence would still be there, unchanged. Both were keyed to his life force, they would stand so long as he lived.

Home, he was home! He looked around him, relishing the sight of his own plane, his own place. How could he have thought to give this up for a mere mortal? This was where he belonged, nowhere else. He'd been foolish to think he would ever be happy anywhere else, being anything but what he was. Alistair, son of Anoch and Molla, was home.

He opened his fist, stared down at the medallion that had bound him for so long. It still had terrible power over him, but now he was home he would take it to his father, a daemon strong enough to destroy it forever. He snarled as he looked closely at the grotesque engraving for the first time. Keri had known it was there, and she'd lied to him, kept him bound to that bed and to her. Alistair threw back his head and roared in pain and rage, the walls trembling at the sound.

It didn't take long for his family to sense his return. His mother had always had a powerful bond with her children, and the moment he crossed the threshold of his home he knew she would be able to feel his return. She arrived after only a few minutes, her pale hair in disarray and her bare feet making almost no sound as she ran across the room and threw her arms around him, hugging him tightly. "My son, you have come back to us."

"Yes Mother, I am home." He had to laugh as his mother's emotions spilled over into a physical display of shimmering light that surrounded them both. "I missed you." He admitted through the lump in his throat. "I have missed you all."

"By Styx woman, dampen the glow!" A booming voice filled the room they were in. "Or are you trying to blind him his first day back with us?" A massive hand clapped down on Alistair's back, knocking him forward a step. "I was starting to think you had forgotten the way home son."

Alistair released his mother and turned to face his sire, bracing himself just in time to absorb most of the impact of the bear hug he was wrapped in.

"I came home as soon as I could." He slapped his father on the back several times in greeting. "I have a great deal to tell you, and not much time."

Anoch released his son and nodded. "What happened to you boy? Where have you been?"

Alistair opened his hand and revealed the medallion to his parents. "I've been a prisoner."

Molla hissed in distaste at the medallion while her mate growled in fury.

"Sorcery." They both spoke at once.

"What did I tell you about sorcerers?" Anoch looked from the medallion to his son and back, a deep scowl on his face.

"Consider that lesson well learned Father. Very well learned."

"Now isn't the time Anoch." Molla reached out and passed her hand over the disc. "It's still active!" She snatched her hand away as if it burned her. "Destroy it, now!"

Alistair looked to his father and offered him the medallion. "I haven't the power."

The older daemon took it, his fingers curling around the disc as a shimmer of flame engulfed his fist to the wrist. The flames went red, then white, then a brilliant blue and finally faded away. Ash fell from Anoch's hand as he opened his now empty fist.

"It is done." His eyes met Alistair's. "Who did this to you, and where are they now? This isn't finished."

"No, it isn't." Alistair agreed. "I do not know where she is now, but I know where she will be in a few hours." He began to outline his plan.

CHAPTER TEN

She was brewing her second pot of coffee when she heard the rumble of a truck engine outside. Keri went to the window and peeked out, spotting a small cube van with the logo of a national rental agency splashed across its side. Pulling up behind it was a black sports car, and though it was too far away to make out the exact make, it was clearly expensive.

"I hope a seagull uses it for target practice." She muttered to herself as she took a deep breath and went to greet her guests.

The two men that stepped out of the truck were huge. They lumbered up the walk like a pair of steroid pumped bookends, right down to their matching crew cuts. They stopped three feet from the doorway and stepped to each side of the path, giving Keri her first glimpse of Cora. *So that's what a sex kitten looks like.* The thought struck Keri, and she nearly giggled. From the tip of her red polished nails to the toes of her Jimmy Choo sandals, every part of this woman seemed to ooze sex appeal. She was wearing rings that winked and sparkled on almost every finger, and a torque of gold gleamed at her throat, the two ends only an inch or so apart and set with matching red stones Keri had no doubt were rubies.

"Hello there, you must be Keri Anderson. I hope you don't mind my coming by so early." Her dark eyes took Keri's measure with a brief glance. "As I mentioned on the phone, my name is Cora D'Marco."

"It's nice to meet you Ms. D'Marco, and there's no problem with you coming by so early. I was up late with the festivities, but that's nothing a little coffee won't cure." She gestured for the woman to come in. "May I offer you a cup?"

"Thank you but no, I'm fine." She entered, and the two bookends followed her right behind her, filling the entire hallway with their presence. "I hope you don't mind if I get right to business? I'd like to see the bed and confirm it is the one I've been looking for."

"Oh, of course." Keri managed to plaster a smile on her face as she led them down the short hallway to her bedroom. "It's in here. I'd only just gotten it cleaned up over the weekend."

Cora took one look at the bed and her painted lips curved into a predatory smile. "That's it." She stepped past Keri as if she weren't even there and walked around the bed, running her hands over the carvings with an almost seductive caress. "Oh yes." She purred. "This is what I've been looking for."

"Well if it belongs to your family, then I couldn't possibly keep it from you." Keri gestured to the bed. "It's beautiful, but it wouldn't be right for me to have it."

Cora paused and glanced over her shoulder as if only just remembering Keri was there. "Oh, that's very considerate. I'd like to offer you double what you paid, to make up for the restoration and the inconvenience."

Keri blinked. "Double? Well, that would be very generous. Uh, thank you."

The sorceress merely made a dismissive gesture with one manicured hand and turned back to the bed. "Archer, Hunter come."

Both men stepped forward and joined their mistress by the bed. "Dismantle this, carefully. I don't want a single scratch."

"Yes ma'am," they replied in unison.

Now that's a little creepy.

As the two started taking the bed apart, Cora flashed a smile that sent a chill running down Keri's spine. "Let's leave the boys to their work shall we?" The woman walked right past Keri and out into the hall, clearly expecting her to follow. She made her way to the living room and turned around, her expression now far from friendly. "So, where is it?"

For a moment Keri was truly confused. "Where's what?"

Cora's expression grew darker, "The medallion that was fastened to the top of the bedpost. Where is it?"

Her mouth suddenly felt like it was stuffed with cotton. "Medallion? I don't know what you mean. The bed came just like you see it."

Cora sighed. "It really does you no good to lie to me. I can still sense him you know. Oh, he's gone now, but he hasn't been gone very long." Dark eyes locked on Keri's and seemed to see right into her soul. "We were together far too long for me not to know the taste of his energy, and he left it *all* over you."

"I don't know w-what you're talking about." Keri stammered.

"Liar." Cora's voice was glacier cold. "When he bedded you, did he make you feel like you were the only woman in the world? Did you scream out his name and beg him to take you again? I am sure you did. They all did. I watched him so many times, with so many women. He was very good at making them feel special and then making them scream."

"No."

"Lying again? You really shouldn't bother. You aren't very good at deception."

Cora crossed the room and stroked Keri's cheek, a sensuous caress that made Keri cringe, but when she tried to look away, she found herself paralyzed, unable to move.

He seduced you and got you to free him, didn't he?" Cora's voice was low and sultry, the words sliding into Keri's brain and holding her attention captive. "He was always so good with the ladies, charming them into doing anything he wanted. And oh, the things he did to them. Some of them were never the same." The sorceress shook her head sadly. "So charming, and so dangerous. I kept him locked up to keep women like you safe."

"No, you kept him a prisoner so you could toy with him, use him." Keri snapped back. A vision of a pair of heavy metal doors slamming shut filled her mind, and suddenly Cora's words were only words, no longer enthralling her.

The dark haired sorceress laughed at her. "Oh ho! The kitten has claws, how amusing. Did he even notice you were gifted, little sister? Or was he too busy feeding on your pleasure to realize what you are?"

Keri took a step back, confused. "What are you talking about now?"

"You, of course, don't you know what you are?" Cora laughed harder. "You don't, do you? You don't know, and he didn't notice. I'd have thought he was smarter than that. I wonder how you managed to free him if neither of you—" She shrugged. "That's a puzzle for another time."

Cora lifted her voice and called for the two men. "Now, since you are resistant to my charms little sister, we have two choices remaining. Either you tell me where that medallion is, or I have my boys convince you to."

A pair of massive hands curled around Keri's upper arms, holding her in an iron grip. "I really, really think you should tell me now. Alistair was the first daemon I captured, but he wasn't the last. Archer and his brother aren't incubi, though, they feed on pain, not pleasure."

The grip on Keri's arms tightened, and she knew she'd have bruises where his fingers were biting into her flesh. "I'm not telling you anything. I owe him that much."

"Very well, have it your way." Cora shrugged. "But believe me, he's not worth what is about to happen to you." She stepped back and began to chant, and suddenly Keri could hear nothing at all, despite the fact Cora's lips were still moving.

One of the daemons stepped in front of her, she wasn't sure which one but she did notice that he was no longer hiding what he was. His eyes were now red with black irises, and there were crimson horns curling back over his head. He leered at her, flashing a mouthful of sharp teeth. He reached out for her with a clawed hand and shredded her shirt as he tore it from her body, leaving her dressed in nothing but tattered shreds of cloth from the waist up.

Keri screamed in terror, but even as she felt the air leaving her lungs the silence remained. She screamed again, and she could see the daemon in front of her laughing, but she still couldn't hear a thing. *Another spell, well, so much for screaming for help.*

With terrible clarity, she realized what the price for Alistair's freedom would be. *I'm going to die, and it's going to hurt.* She closed her eyes and prayed to whatever powers were listening that Alistair was safe, and wherever he was, he'd found a way to completely free himself from Cora's magic. If she'd only told him right away, maybe things would have been different. But she hadn't, and he was gone, and there was no way she would betray his trust again. Cora had already stolen too much of his life, Keri was going to make sure he lived the rest of it in peace.

She felt talons on her skin, five sharp points resting just above her bare breast, holding there for just a moment before sinking in deep. Even past the pain she could feel her own blood well up and trickle down her skin as she screamed again, twisting away from the hurt he was inflicting.

Behind her, the other one shifted slightly, and she felt something sharp tear into her shoulder. She knew without looking he'd bitten her, and she choked back another silent scream of pain as black and red spots began to dance behind her eyelids.

* * * *

Alistair shifted a few seconds before his family, letting them focus on his energy to ensure they would be able to follow him to the right place, the deck just outside Keri's bedroom. The moment he arrived he could feel his skin itch with the presence of magic; Cora was already here. Part of his mind registered the partially dismantled bed, and he felt his heart twist as he realized in his rage at her betrayal he'd left Keri to face his worst enemy all alone. He broke into a run as the others materialized around him.

When he reached the limit of his former prison he hesitated, some part of him still expecting to meet the barrier that had always held him back. Then he heard his father's footsteps behind him and kept going. Things were different this time, everything was different. When he rounded the corner into the living room he came to a skidding halt as his senses registered the scene in front of him.

"Keri!" He roared her name and felt a surge of power behind it, shattering the silence spell that cloaked the room.

Keri hung on the talons of a Daemon, her blood bright against the terrible pallor of her skin. When she heard Alistair's voice, he saw her struggle to lift her head, her pretty eyes dull with pain and shock as she finally saw him. "No!" She croaked, her voice so raw and hoarse it made his heart ache for her. "I wanted you to be safe!"

"Oh how sweet, you came back for your pet." Cora purred from her spot on the couch. "And here I thought I was going to have to leave here empty handed."

"Let her go!" Alistair's voice was a low growl of fury as he glowered at the two young daemons holding Keri.

One of them drew back his teeth and snarled. Alistair's rage burned hot, and he roared in fury. They had made his Keri bleed and suffer. They were going to die. He charged the one whose hands were covered in her blood, hitting him hard enough he felt ribs break as he sent the younger daemon flying across the room.

He followed his prey across the room, hauling him up from the floor and shaking him like a terrier would a rat. "You serve that bitch? Then die a traitor to your race." He raged at the terrified daemon that scratched and scrabbled at the hand locked around his throat. Alistair kept squeezing, depriving the other daemon of air until he stopped fighting and slumped to the floor. Without hesitation, Alistair stepped over him, reached down and snapped his neck before tossing the body away with disdain. There was a crunch, and the corpse of the second daemon landed on the coffee table nearby, crushing it. He glanced up and met the eyes of his father who greeted him with teeth bared in a savage smile.

"Now we deal with her," Anoch growled and pointed to Cora, screaming and fighting a golden-haired daemon that had her backed into a corner.

When they approached the others in the room gave way, and the blonde daemon grinned over his shoulder as he saw them arrive. "She doesn't seem to want to see you again brother."

"It would appear not Malyk, despite her coming all this way to find me." Alistair greeted his half-brother as he yanked the still screaming Cora to the center of the room.

* * * *

Keri saw Alistair and her heart had shattered. He was supposed to be safe! This was her penance for lying to him, why was he here? The hold on her arms suddenly loosened and she staggered forward, barely able to stand on her own without the daemon's grip keeping her upright.

From behind her she heard a booming voice snarl something in a language, she didn't understand, and then she was falling, crashing to the floor as the room spun around her and everything went black.

When she came back to her senses, Keri didn't know exactly what was happening, but she knew enough to get out of the way. She crawled towards the nearest corner as her living room seemed to fill with people, all of them angry and growling. She heard raised voices and a whimper of pain, then the crunch of wood giving way. *There goes the coffee table,* part of her noted with an inward sigh of resignation. She kept crawling until she found herself huddled against the wall, her knees drawn up to her chest as she desperately scanned the room, looking for Alistair.

She spotted him at last, his anger a nearly tangible thing as he stood in the center of a circle of daemons of all descriptions. Beside him was another daemon whose similar appearance and aura of power marked him as Alistair's sire. Between them stood Cora, her arms pinned to her sides by Alistair's firm grip. Cora's eyes were wide with fear as she stared around her, her entire demeanor cloaked in misery and defeat.

Keri felt a gentle touch on her shoulder and startled, flinching away from the contact out of instinct.

"It's alright child, I will not harm you." A voice as soft as summer rain soothed her, and she turned to find the source, coming face to face with the most beautiful woman she had ever seen. Her hair was as pale as moonlight, and her eyes were a familiar shade of golden brown. "You are the one who freed my son, yes?"

Keri nodded, unsure what to even say when faced with an angel.

"I'm Molla, mother to Alistair and mate to Anoch." She nodded to the two standing together in the circle. "You were hurt trying to protect him from her?"

"I wouldn't tell her where he was," Keri whispered, wincing at the discomfort even that soft sound caused. "He should have stayed away, she's too dangerous."

Molla made a small sound of comfort and carefully draped a shawl of pale silk over Keri's shoulders and the shredded remains of her clothes. "For Alistair alone, it would be too dangerous. But my son is not alone, he has family who loves him and has tried to find him for a long time. We would still be looking if it weren't for you." She leaned in and pressed a motherly kiss to Keri's cheek, the warmth of it spreading throughout her body. As the warmth faded, the pain did too.

Keri's hands flew to the wounds on her chest, amazed to find them healed over. "Thank you!"

"You were hurt protecting my son, the least I could do was heal you of that pain. Now watch, and you will see you need never fear the sorceress again."

Keri's attention returned Cora, and she realized that Anoch was speaking.

"...and in that you have been found guilty of imprisoning a Prince of the House of Anoch, practicing enchantments against the citizens of the plane of Daemos, and generally being an utter bitch; I hereby strip you of all your stolen years and banish your soul to the void between the planes to drift for eternity."

Alistair grinned as he stepped into Cora's line of vision. "The first hundred years are the worst, after that, it gets easier."

Cora screamed and fell to her knees, a babble of words falling from her mouth as she begged for forgiveness, for mercy, for a chance to make amends. But then her voice cracked, and her words became a keening wail. As the others watched she aged, so rapidly it seemed she was shrinking down on herself, within a matter of seconds, her body crumbled away to dust, leaving only her jewels and clothing behind.

"And that's the end of that," Anoch announced and gripped his son by the shoulder. "She is gone, never to touch one of mine again!" The room filled with cheers of approval.

"The party begins in an hour, where we shall welcome my son home properly." A louder cheer this time, and then the room went quickly silent as the crowd vanished one by one, returning to their own plane.

Soon there were only five of them left in the room, Alistair, Malyk, his parents, and Keri. Anoch crossed the room and helped his mate to her feet before offering a massive hand to Keri.

"You have returned my son to me, for that you have my thanks." He smiled down at Keri with an expression she had seen on Alistair's face often enough the similarity hurt. She knew that smile, and she also knew Alistair would never look at her that way again.

"I should have done more." She murmured as she stood up slowly, her free hand gripping the shawl to keep herself decently covered.

"Perhaps." Anoch glanced over to where he son stood alone, his back to the rest of them. "That is not for me to judge, though."

Keri blinked as a blonde daemon stepped into her line of vision and smiled at her, his eyes the same pale golden brown as Molla's. "I am Malyk. Thank you for bringing our brother back to us. What you have done will not be forgotten."

Keri looked up at Malyk and smiled faintly, doing her best to ignore the lump in her throat and the ache in her heart. "I am glad he's going home at last."

Malyk frowned and glanced at his brother, then back to Keri. "I see." Sadness gleamed in his eyes for a moment and then he stepped away. "I will take my leave. Be well Keri."

Before she could answer Malyk he was gone, and Molla's voice chimed softly from behind her.

"Hold still a moment."

Keri felt the touch of metal at the back of her neck, and then a strange tingle passed through her body, and a weight settled around her throat. When her fingers reached up, she realized she was now wearing Cora's gold torque.

"Consider that a thank you gift." Molla stepped back to Keri's side and adjusted the necklace so that the two ends sat just over her collar bone. "It cannot be removed by mortal hands, so I hope you like it." Her voice fluted with laughter as she met Anoch's surprised gaze. "I know mate, but there is a reason, you will have to trust me."

Anoch just laughed and took Molla's hand. "Very well, but later you are going to explain to me your reasons." They both returned to Alistair and said a brief goodbye, and then they were gone, leaving the two of them alone.

The moment they left Alistair turned his back to her and stared out the window. "I'm glad my mother healed you. It was never my intention that you be hurt. I didn't consider what she would do if she realized you had freed me. Whatever else there is between us Keri, I would never wish you harm." His shoulders were tense, and he held himself rigid as he stood with his hands fisted at his sides, his face still turned away from her.

"I didn't think of it either, not until she point-blank asked me where the medallion was and told me she knew you hadn't been gone long." Keri took a step towards him and stopped, wishing he'd turn around, wanting to see his face. "I'm glad you are free." She finally whispered, fighting back tears.

"I want you to take her jewelry, not just the torque my parents gave to you, all of it. It will pay for any damages done to your home. And buy you a new bed."

"A new bed?" She asked, confused again.

"Two of my kin were assigned to destroy it before leaving. You'll need a new one. Try to find something without an enchantment on it this time."

"Thanks, I'll try." Keri heard the faintest note of humor in his voice and took courage enough from that to cross the room, coming to stand at his side.

"I'll miss you." Her heart slammed and leaped into her throat as she whispered her confession.

He glanced down at her, his anger and guilt clearly visible as he took in the blood on her newly healed skin, the marks still pink where they showed beneath the sheer material of his mother's shawl.

He looked away again, his jaw tightening. "I know you'll miss me. You wanted to keep me a prisoner, clearly you enjoyed my company."

Keri cringed at his words, knowing she deserved them. She saw the set of his jaw and knew he couldn't forgive her, not after what she'd done. Her heart broke as she realized he was going to leave her, just like everyone else did. She mustered the last of her courage and lifted her gaze to his face. "I know you can't forgive me, but I am sorry for what I did. You should go home to your family, they're all waiting for you."

She turned away and started walking, willing herself not to cry until he was gone. She glanced back to look at him one last time, but the room was empty. "Goodbye, Alistair." She whispered and then finally let herself cry.

CHAPTER ELEVEN

It had been three weeks since Alistair had left and she was constantly haunted by the memories of their brief time together. The deck, the bedroom, even the bathroom conjured up images of them together; laughing, loving and enjoying each other. *How could someone make such a hole in my heart after only a few days?* She asked herself that question over and over again, but she already knew the answer. She loved him. She loved him, and she'd lost him, and if anyone tried to tell her that it was better than to have loved and lost than never to have loved at all she was going to hit them upside the head with a very heavy brick.

She'd stopped sleeping in her bedroom after the first night, the king sized mattress felt too large, and even with it sitting on the floor she couldn't stop seeing the carved columns of Alistair's bed rising up around her. She'd tried sleeping on the couch for another week, but now she was barely sleeping at all. Her nightmares had gotten worse, until every time she closed her eyes she was back on that beach, running. It was easier to push herself to the point of exhaustion, then collapse for a few hours until the dream woke her and she started the cycle again.

She'd reclaimed her grandmother's workshop and made it her own; cleaning out the space, sharpening the tools and restoring the place to order. When that was done, she'd started carving, not even sure what she was doing at first, just that she needed to keep busy. The first bedpost had been carved before she'd even known what she was going to make, but now she was on a mission. She was going to make her own bed to replace the one that had been destroyed, one that was untouched by magic or darkness or memories. She hoped that maybe when it was complete, she could sleep again. That maybe her heart would have started healing by then.

The carvings were like nothing she'd done before; the four posts would be tree trunks, rising up to a canopy of branches that interlaced overhead. The headboard was already roughed out, though it would take hundreds of more hours to carve in the details of the meadow that would cover it when it was done. Every flower she could imagine, she would carve into the wood. The task consumed her; she ate only when she remembered to and slept when she was too tired to continue.

Samantha dropped by almost daily to check on her, bringing her out sandwiches and trying to cajole Keri out of her workshop and back into the world. She'd only asked once about Keri's whirlwind courtship, and when she had burst into tears, Samantha had hugged her close and not mentioned it again. Keri knew what few friends she had were all worried, but work was how she always dealt with grief, and until it stopped hurting she could see no reason to stop.

A reason finally appeared one day as she wandered out of the bathroom. Scrubbed and pink after taking a long overdue shower she'd spotted something through the half open door to the second bedroom; a room she hadn't bothered to enter in weeks. There on the dresser, right where she'd left it, was the tapestry she had bought the day Alistair had appeared. She'd completely forgotten about it. She unrolled it carefully and admired it, her fingers brushing over the images formed in the wool, her artist's eye already looking at the lines and wondering how to incorporate them into her carving.

As she touched one twisted arbutus tree, she gasped and finally saw what her subconscious had known the moment she'd laid eyes on it back at the market. "It's my dream!" She couldn't believe it. "That's the beach in my dreams!" There was no mistaking it now she had seen it, the trees, the rocks, even the curve of the shoreline exactly matched the one she'd been dreaming about for months.

She raced to her car, nothing in her mind but the need to go, to see it for herself. Her car protested every curve of the road with a squeal of tires as she drove far too fast for the twists and hills the road traversed, trying to recall the directions the weaver had given her about how to get to the beach. She wasn't even sure why she needed to go, but there was no arguing with the feeling that drove her, she had to see it for herself.

She reached the spot the woman had described and pulled over to the side of the road, throwing up a spray of gravel as she came to a stop and scrambled to get out of the car. *There!* She spotted the unmarked trailhead, little more than a slight gap in the trees and undergrowth and headed for it. The trail was rough, uneven and dark, the evergreen canopy blocking out most of the sunlight. She tripped over a tree root and yelped in pain, only then realizing that in her hurry she hadn't even changed out of her summer sandals and into a pair of decent walking shoes.

When she reached the beach it took her a minute to get her bearings, but then she saw a familiar rock outcropping off to her left, and she went towards it, kicking off her nearly useless shoes in favor of walking barefoot through the sand.

Now that she was here, she felt oddly at peace, the insistent voice that had that had pushed her to come here having faded away somewhere during her descent to the water.

Her summer dress fluttered against her calves as she wandered down the beach and the breeze lifted her hair and blew it around her face in a playful halo. Thoughts and feelings she had pushed aside came back to her, and for the first time in weeks she found herself thinking clearly about her life, about Alistair, about everything.

Like the images in the tapestry, she started to see her life from a different viewpoint, saw the pattern of fear that had repeated itself over and over. Every time things had grown difficult, she had retreated into her fear and let it rule her. Ever since her father had died, it had been the same. Fear, withdrawal, and then when she had lost the thing she'd fear to lose it had confirmed yet again that nothing lasted, that everyone left. It was a self-fulfilling prophecy.

The understanding of that froze her in her tracks. She had made it happen, pushed people away, maybe not every time, but often enough. "Not anymore," She vowed, a sense of determination growing with every step.

She'd lost track of time as she walked, and when her revelations were complete, she looked around and realized she'd gone more than a mile down the beach. While she'd been wandering the weather had changed, and the tide had turned, and now it was coming in, fast. She turned around and started jogging back, quickly realizing she was at risk of being cut off by the tide, stranded and barefoot on the wrong side of the beach. The waves were rolling in faster now, and the wind whipped up as the sun vanished behind a line of dark clouds. "Oh no," Keri moaned as she recognized the coming storm and doubled her speed, a sense of dread filling her.

Sprinting now, she moved too fast to avoid the rocks and shells that lay buried in the sand. Just like in her dreams they cut at her feet, slowing her down. There were differences, though, and she hung onto those differences in hopes they meant escape was possible, a way that wouldn't end in her death. Before she'd always been running away, running further down the beach towards some unknown thing that she needed to find. Not this time. This time, she knew what she had lost and was running back to reclaim it. If she could only get back home, she'd find a way to make it right. She ran faster.

Her lungs burned as she pushed herself past the fear and the pain. *She was going to make it back, back to her life, back to her art, and if she could find a way, back to Alistair.* She hung onto that thought until the wind tossed up a salt spray of sea foam that blinded her, and with a sinking heart, she felt hope fade. The nightmare was going to end the same way, only this time there would be no waking up.

She closed her eyes and thought of Alistair, her heart crying out his name as she realized she'd never see him again, never get a chance to explain. Grief and regret flooded her that she'd figured everything out too late. "I'm sorry." She whispered into the rising wind as the roar of the wave grew deafening. "Maybe in my next life I'll get it right."

The rogue wave slammed into the shore, obliterating the beach where she'd been standing only minutes before. She stood and stared in shock as the water surged to the tree line and then fell back into the sea. It had missed her.

* * * *

It had been three weeks since the medallion had been destroyed and he should have been glorying in his freedom, but he wasn't happy. The joy of being home had faded within days, as had the sense of satisfaction at knowing Cora had been defeated and destroyed.

His one joy was spending time with his family, but they had their own lives and schedules to keep. When he was not with them, he was alone, and it felt as though he were back in his prison again.

Alistair paced through his home, the furnishings, and valuables he had yearned to return to unseen as he wandered from room to room. He missed Keri. So much so he hadn't been able to feed since he had been freed. He'd tried twice, and both times he'd failed to make the most preliminary of connections, leaving their mortal dreams as quietly as he had entered them. Both women had been beautiful and as ripe as sweet plums for the picking, but he'd not been tempted at all. He ran a hand through his hair and growled in frustration. "Why can't I stop thinking about her?"

A soft riff of laughter sounded from behind him, and he spun around, startled. When he spotted his mother's diminutive form nestled into one chair near the fireplace he relaxed and greeted her with a sarcastic, "Do make yourself at home Mother."

"It's been weeks my son, and you are still so unsettled. I decided it was time for mother-son talk." She patted the chair beside hers in invitation.

"I've been gone a long time, but I'm certain it's still considered polite for visitors to knock first when they come over uninvited." He grumbled as he took a seat beside her.

"Mothers get special privileges." Molla laid a soft hand on his arm. "I know you're unhappy, what's wrong?"

"I can't stop thinking about Keri." The words came out before he could stop them. "I don't understand why, though. She lied to me, tried to keep me prisoner. Why can't I forget about her?"

"Really Alistair, three weeks of asking yourself that question and you haven't found the answer yet? My son, you surprise me. I thought you were smarter than this."

He bristled. "I'm smart enough to know she's mortal and a liar.

I remember enough of my teaching to recall that daemons and mortals are not suited to more than a few nights of passion."

"If you recall, the Elders also claim that your parents could never be happy together, and you should never have been born. We all make mistakes son, daemons and mortals alike. I think you're focusing on the wrong thing. The fact that she hid the medallion's existence from you isn't the issue. You need to ask yourself why she did it."

"I know why she did it. She wanted to keep me with her, to force me to stay." Alistair shrugged. "It's pretty clear to me."

Molla threw up her hands in frustration. "You are just like your father. He didn't want to accept reality either. I had hoped you'd get a bit more of my intuition, but it seems you are your father's son."

"What am I missing?" Alistair blinked at his mother.

"Your father came up with a hundred reasons why we couldn't be together after he bedded me. It took me a year to wear him down." Molla smiled at the memories. "He was the most stubborn, thick headed daemon I had ever met. But I knew we were meant to be together, and I made him see it too." She cocked her head to smile at Alistair. "Or did you believe his claims that it was love at first sight, and he carried me off the first night we met, never to let me out of his sight again?"

Alistair gave his mother a stunned look. "Actually, I did believe him, but that's not the issue right now. I am not making excuses! Even if there was a reason she did it, and I forgave her for the lies, she's human! You know why that never works for us!"

Molla sighed. "I had forgotten how young you were when we lost you. You wouldn't know what to look for. Alistair, she's not human, not completely. Couldn't you feel it?"

"I felt...something." He gave his mother a wild-eyed look.

"And she had prophetic dreams, but that doesn't necessarily mean anything. Does it?"

She nodded. "In this case, it does. Her power is quite impressive, but no one has taught her how to use it. Your Keri is a cambion. And more importantly, she loves you."

"No, she doesn't." He started to argue, but his mother held up her hand to stop him.

"Your brother Malyk and I both felt it the day we destroyed Cora. She loves you very much, and your leaving hurt her more than anything those daemons did to her."

Alistair cringed at the idea he'd hurt Keri, but at the same time, his pulse raced as he realized what his mother was telling him. She loved him, and there was a chance for them to be together. "So she could survive the journey between planes?"

"Yes, with you to guide her she'd be fine. Now, will you please go find her and sort this out between you? I've done everything I can, but there are some things you really must do for yourself." Molla stood and kissed Alistair's cheek. "Go."

He had to find Keri. Alistair was moving between the planes before he'd even finished standing, his mind reaching out, searching for her. He'd been a fool, letting his anger blind him to what was really important.

He stepped through the veil and into her bedroom, but there was nothing but a bare mattress leaning up against the wall. She wasn't sleeping here anymore, that was clear. "Keri!" He called her name as he moved through the house, but she wasn't there. He was nearly to the front door when her voice filled his head, her fear ripping through him. He followed Keri's voice back through the veil without thinking, not even sure how he could be doing it. He appeared behind her just in time to see the wave slam into the shore and hear her softly spoken hopes for her next life.

Then he had her in his arms, held tight against his chest, her sweet softness everything he remembered in their weeks apart.

Alistair's leaned down and whispered into her ear. "Your next life can wait; I'm not done with you in this life yet."

"You're here." She whispered, her fingers touching his arms where they curved around her as if convincing herself he was really there.

"Aye, I am." He kept his mind on their destination, the realization that she'd been so close to death shaking him to his core. His grip on her tightened, and he finished the crossing, both of them materializing at the threshold of his gate.

* * * *

The moment they stopped moving Alistair had spun her around and cupped her face in his hands. "Open your eyes, Keri."

She did and found herself staring up into his golden brown eyes. "Why?" She didn't dare to even breathe as she waited for his answer.

"Why should you open your eyes? So I could see for myself you were alright. I nearly lost you back there." His fingertips brushed over her cheek.

"No, why did you come back at all? I thought you hated me for what I did."

He groaned and leaned down into their noses were nearly touching. "I do not hate you. I couldn't hate you. By Styx woman, I *need* you." He dropped his lips to hers and kissed her, his fingers sliding into her hair and tangling in her red tresses, holding her mouth to his as he plundered it. She shuddered and then melted into his embrace with a faint sigh.

Her pulse leaped like a startled deer as he kissed her and hope kindled in her heart. She threw her arms around his neck and clung to him as she kissed him back.

Her lips parted beneath his, and she moaned as his tongue slipped into her mouth to dance with hers. One hand remained buried in her hair while his other moved down to cup her ass, lifting her up off her feet and against his hard body as he moved her backward until she was pinned up against a wall.

Alistair whispered her name as he lifted her higher, settling his hips into the cradle of her thighs. Each time she moaned she felt him grind his rock hard cock against her, which drew another moan. Soon they were both half wild with need from the game they were playing, and she wrapped her legs around his hips, determined to never let go of him again. Her nails curled into his shoulders, and she pulled him closer still, needing to feel every inch of him. She felt a faint tug as he used her hair to draw her head to one side, baring her throat. She tipped her head further, offering herself to him. His lips found her pulse point, sucking on her soft skin. Rough palms slid up her thighs, shoving her skirt aside.

He groaned against her skin, grinding his hips into her again and again as he reached for her panties, shredding the already damp lace that covered her mound. His thumb slid into her folds, unerringly finding that small pearl of pleasure and rubbing hard against it. She mewled in pleasure, and he shifted his hand, sliding a finger deep inside her. Keri writhed against him, wanting more. Her vaginal walls closed around his finger, and she gasped as his fingertip brushed near the sensitive cluster of nerves within her channel.

"Please." She whimpered and bucked her hips against his hand.

Her soft whimper drew a nod of agreement from him, and he slid another finger inside, then a third, stretching and stroking her as his thumb toyed mercilessly her clit. "Come for me Keri, I want to see you come." He curled his long fingers, hitting the one spot he knew would bring her to the brink.

Her womb clenched, and she cried out as her orgasm took her, his fingers still moving, dragging out her release. She turned her head and pressed an open-mouthed kiss to his neck, her tongue drawing over his skin, tasting him before her teeth closed on his flesh. She felt him tense from the bite, and a faint smile curved her lips. "Now I want to see you come." She purred.

"As my lady wishes." His fingers withdrew from her body, and she felt his clothes vanish, leaving nothing between them. His lips found hers, and he kissed her hard, groaning into her mouth as his thick shaft breached her body. His claimed her with a single thrust, his hips already moving before either of them could catch their breath, setting a demanding rhythm.

Keri gripped her thighs tighter, drawing him close, needing him to fill her. Her nails dug deeper into his shoulder as she hung onto him, her lips still locked with his. He sucked on her lower lip, drawing it into his mouth, his teeth nibbling at her kiss swollen skin as his hips arched higher, driving himself deeper still.

Keri moaned again as a new sensation swirled within her, making her giddy. An odd pulse of liquid heat filled her, and a rich flavor filled her mouth, the taste of spiced honey and musk. His taste, his scent. She clung to him, lost in her pleasure. In and out, in and out, she felt her release building with every thrust as he made wild love to her.

She sensed his control slip, felt the frenzied way his body moved against hers, taking everything she offered without quarter. He tore his lips from hers and threw his head back, roaring his claim to the world. "She's MINE!"

They came together, both of them calling the other's name as they found their release. She let herself relax into the strength of his arms, her head dropping onto his chest as a final shudder of exquisite bliss passed through her.

Stepping back from the wall, she felt him lift her, separating their bodies and letting her head rest on his shoulder as he carried her to a chair, seating himself and then settling her into his lap. "Keri." He crooned her name, his lips near hear ear. "Come back to me Love."

She stirred, her eyes opening slowly. "I'm not going anywhere, not ever again." She smiled up at him. "I just feel a bit strange is all." For the first time, she took a good look around them. "Where are we anyway? This isn't my house."

"No, it's mine."

"But yours is—that isn't—" She stammered, confused. "How?"

"It was brought to my attention by someone much smarter than me, that you are more than you appear to be my Beauty. I told you that no human could survive the journey between planes. Since you're here, and you are most definitely alive, I'd say there's a good chance you're not entirely human."

"What?" Keri tried to sit up and found herself held fast in Alistair's arms. "Say that again. Slowly."

"You. Are. Not. Human." Alistair sounded out each word as he visibly struggled not to laugh out loud at her confusion. "According to my mother, you're a cambion."

"Oh." Keri uttered that single syllable and then went silent for a few minutes. "I sure hope we're not related."

He gave in at last and burst out laughing. When he finally stopped, he cupped her cheek and said, "I tell you that you're not human, and the first worry you have is that we're kin? My Beauty, you amaze me. No, we're not related.

My family pay great attention to our children and their lineage, you are not from my house. "

"Well, that's good." She laid her hand on his bare chest, over his heart. "You still haven't answered my question, though. Why did you come back?"

"A better question might be, why did I leave you at all." He replied, his voice soft and tinged with regret.

"I know the answer to that one, though. I lied to you about the medallion. I wanted one more day with you, one perfect memory I could hold onto after you had gone. It was wrong of me, and I'm sorry."

"That's not the whole answer Love. You lied, and I was angry. But when saw how brave you'd been, refusing to tell Cora anything, I should have realized you would never be like her. The real reason I left was because I didn't want to admit I was in love with a mortal."

Keri's eyes widened, and her lip reappeared as she smiled. "You are huh?"

"Yes minx, I am. And it's my great hope that she's in love with me too, because if not, things are going to get rather awkward."

"She is! I mean I am!" She laughed and kissed him. "I have no idea how this is all going to work, but I love you too. I realized today that

193

I wanted to be with you, no matter what the risks. I'm tired of being afraid to live my life the way I want it to be."

"Thank Styx for that." He held her close and kissed her again before adding, "It seems we both had some decisions to make it."

"Decisions!" Keri gasped. "Samantha said I'd need to make choices soon, and my life would change once I made them. And then today on the beach I turned around and tried to get back home, to find a way to tell you what I wanted. It was just like my nightmares Alistair, but this time, I was running the other way, and the wave missed me. I changed the outcome! I've never been able to do that before."

"I'm glad you did. If I had lost you, I don't know if I could have survived it." He laid his hand over hers where it still rested over his heart.

"But you didn't lose her." Keri nearly leaped out of Alistair's arms as another woman's voice joined their conversation.

"Mother! Will you stop doing that!" Alistair snapped as Molla stepped into the room. "Why can't you use the door, just once?"

"Where would the fun be in that?" Anoch asked as he followed his wife into the room. "Get dressed boy, I don't need to see that!"

Alistair conjured his clothing and smoothed Keri's dress back over her legs, his hand holding her in place when she tried to get up from his lap. "If you used the door like everyone else, you wouldn't have to see it."

"Point taken." Anoch seated his wife and himself and then grinned at the young couple. "Keri, it's good to see you again. Molla and I were starting to wonder if our son was ever going to get himself sorted out." He gave a snort of laughter. "My mate has informed me he takes after me in such matters."

Molla shook her head. "Not nearly so hopeless as you were as it turns out. He claimed his mate within a month. You took a year."

Keri frowned, confused. "Mate?"

Anoch saw her expression and chuckled long and hard before asking, "You didn't ask her first? Have you not told her what you have done?"

"I was getting to it." Alistair glowered at his parents. "But someone interrupted us."

"What are you all talking about?" Keri asked firmly.

"When we were, uh, busy a moment ago, I did something I hadn't intended to do before asking."

Molla elbowed her mate in the ribs as he chuckled again. "Hush you, let him finish."

Keri gave Alistair her best narrow-eyed stare. "What did you do?"

"I claimed you as my mate."

"What? How? Why does every conversation we have today start with me asking you to explain something! Alistair, what does that mean?"

He silenced her with a kiss and then gestured to his parents. "The reason they are here is because they heard my claim. My whole family did." He drew a deep breath and then grinned. "In human terms, we're married."

"You're kidding," Keri let that information sink in. "So that's it? I'm yours? Don't I get a say?"

"Of course, you do Keri." Molla chimed in softly. "If you don't want this then all you have to do is say so. He's claimed you as his own, but you do not have to agree to it." Molla arched a brow. "He seems to have gotten ahead of himself, another trait he got from his father."

"I see." Keri turned her hand and wove her fingers with Alistair's, squeezing them tight. "That was the worst proposal I have ever heard of. I hope you intend to make it up to me later."

"Is that a yes?" Alistair asked.

"That's a yes." She laughed, her heart nearly overflowing with happiness. She glanced over at Anoch and Molla. "So long as you do not mind that your son is mated to a mortal."

"Oh, you're not mortal my daughter." Molla beamed at them. "Not so long as you're wearing that torque I gave you."

Keri's free hand reached up to touch the gold band around her neck. "I don't understand."

"That torque was the source of Cora's youth and vitality. How she came to possess it, I am not sure, but it's a very powerful bit of jewelry. It allows the wearer to absorb the sexual energy of others and use it to sustain their own life force."

"You mean she can..." Alistair blinked and stared at Keri, hope glowing in his golden eyes.

"She can." Molla nodded. "Keri has latent powers of her own, enough that she can use the necklace even without training. Keri, that torque will let you live as long as you wish, so long as you do not remove it. Like Cora, you will need to feed on sexual energy from time to time, but given that you are now mated to my son, I do not think that will be an issue."

Keri blushed at Molla's pointed observation. "Um, thank you."

Her arms lifted and wound around Alistair's neck. "So I'm now a married, part daemon without an expiry date. Does that sum up what just happened here?"

Alistair bowed his head until his lips were nearly brushing hers and smiled. "That about covers it, Love."

She kissed him then, a tender kiss full of hope as her new in-laws laughed in approval.

"I believe that's our cue to leave." Anoch stood, drawing his mate up and then scooping her into his arms. "You can thank me for this later. If I don't take her out now, she'll be here all day helping your new mate settle in." He nodded to Keri. "Welcome to the family little one."

"Dinner! You're both invited to dinner!" Molla called as she was carried out.

As they heard the door close Alistair chuckled ruefully, his breath tickling Keri's ear. "My parents are always like that. I'm sorry."

"Are you kidding? That went much better than the last time I met my in-laws." Keri grinned and then gave him a lascivious kiss that had sent all the blood to his groin. "Since we just got married, that means we're on our honeymoon." She whispered the words into his mouth. "So, why aren't we in bed yet?"

CHAPTER TWELVE

"I'll give you the tour later." He informed his new mate as he carried her through the house at a near run, his hands already tearing off her dress and bra, his mouth slanted over hers as he kissed her nearly senseless. He lowered her gently to his bed, immensely satisfied to see her there at last; his mate, his home, his bed. He followed her down to the mattress, relishing the touch of her soft body against his.

As he laid her on his bed, Alistair couldn't stop grinning. He had gained everything he been denied during his long captivity, and more besides. Keri was his, for now, and always. His mate, his world, the reason he would wake every day until time ended. He deftly removed her bra and buried his face into the glorious valley between her breasts, inhaling her scent. "All mine, forever."

He felt her breath catch, a faint tension hardening her soft body.

"Are you sure forever is what you want? You said daemons didn't often take permanent mates."

He lifted his head and gave her a look that was a mix of disbelief and laughter. "Am I sure I wish to spend my life with the woman I can't seem to stop thinking about? By Styx woman, yes I'm sure!"

I couldn't even feed after you freed me. Not once. All I wanted was you."

"Not once?" Relief gleamed in her eyes, and he watched the tension fade away again as her fingers curled gently into his hair. "I thought you would have by now... I'm glad you didn't."

"I didn't, and I won't. No one is coming between us again. You are my mate, now and always." His golden eyes gleamed as he lowered his lips to one nipple, planting a soft kiss on it. "The only one I'm going to feed off is you, and you better not feed off anyone, but me or I'll spank your newly immortal arse."

"You wouldn't dare." She challenged him, wide-eyed and laughing.

"I'm tempted to give you a demonstration right here and now, just to prove it." The image of Keri lying over his thighs sent a flare of heat straight to his groin and his already hard cock turned to steel.

"No!" She yelped as she caught the look in his eyes. "Not a chance daemon boy!"

"Now you're calling me a boy? That's it." He grinned and moved with preternatural speed, rolling them both over and hauling her playfully across his lap, face down.

Keri protested loudly as she tried to wriggle free, every movement sliding their bodies together as she struggled. She finally gave up the fight, panting as her head hung down in defeat. "I'm going to get even with you for this."

"Oh, I hope so." Alistair laughed as his large hand smoothed over one cheek before lifting it and slapping her bare skin. "That is for lying to me about the medallion."

He swatted her again as she started to growl and thrash. "And that is for not believing I would have come back for you after I was freed."

Keri went still. "You said you wanted to go home, that you didn't belong in my world. You were pretty clear about it."

"That was before I got to know you. By Styx woman, give a man a chance to change his mind! Up on the roof, just before the fireworks started I was going to tell you how I felt, but then it was too noisy and before we had another chance to talk you were handing me your phone and all hell broke loose."

His hand stroked over the curve of her ass, soothing the slightly reddened skin where he'd spanked her. "You can spank me for that later, alright?"

"Deal." She twisted her head back to look up at him. "So, can I get up now?"

He swatted her rump once more for good measure and then helped her up as she sputtered at him, loving the fire that glittered in the depths of her eyes when she was riled. The moment she was free she turned and tackled him, landing on top of his chest and pinning him down to the bed as he stared up at her, clearly amused by her actions.

"You are magnificent when you're angry."

Keri just tossed her hair back over her shoulder and glared at him. "Didn't anyone ever warn you about red heads and their tempers?" Without waiting for an answer she turned away from him and twisted herself around until her thighs rested atop his broad chest and she was lying on him, her face resting on the top of his thigh. She bent her knees, lifting her feet into the air and hooking her ankles together, denying him the sight of her sex as she clamped her thighs shut.

"And what are you going to do—" His voice choked off to a strangled groan as she wrapped her fingers around his cock and lowered her mouth to the tip. She began to pump his cock with her fingers, her tongue swirling over the tip, lapping at the pre-cum that appeared almost instantly. When she felt his hands trying to gently pry her knees apart, she resisted.

"Uh-uh." she let the denial vibrate through his rock hard shaft as she took him deep into her mouth.

The same warm sensation washed over her just like before; her senses were filled with the taste and smell of him, spicy and sweet. *His sexual essence,* she realized this was the gift of the torque she wore. She experimented, laving his cock quickly with her tongue, her head bobbing in time to the rhythm of her fingers. A shudder passed through Alistair's body, and he groaned loudly, panting now as her mouth edged him closer to the breaking point. Another flood of warmth washed through her, and she reveled in the knowledge she was truly taking a measure of his energy into herself.

"Keri, please." His voice was a raspy groan. "Let me touch you."

She relented, at last, unlocking her ankles and letting her legs slide down his ribs. Her mouth kept working him over, lapping and sucking at his cock as her thighs parted and revealed her labia nearly hidden beneath the trim border of downy red curls

His fingers traced down her seam, resting there lightly as he slid his thumb into her tight passage. "You're so wet, so ready for me." He murmured, moving his thumb in slow circles within her, stretching and teasing.

Keri shuddered with pleasure as he touched her, fighting to keep her mind on what she was doing to him. It was hard to remember anything at all when he was inside her. His thumb pressed deeper, and she moaned around his cock, her fingers loosening of their own accord as her control slipped another notch.

She felt his hands move and then he was holding her hips, pulling her back up his body. Before she could resist his head was between her legs and his tongue was stroking over every inch of her tender flesh. He licked and suckled, drawing her deep into his mouth. He matched the movement of his tongue to hers as she devoured his cock, and the two of them moaned in unison at the pleasures they unleashed in each other.

As though he sensed how close she was, he shifted his hands and entered her with two fingers. His fingers and tongue drove her higher and higher up the scales of passion and Keri knew she was lost. She laved the tip if his cock one last time and lifted her head, drawing a ragged breath into her burning lungs. He arched his fingers and closed his teeth gently around her hardened nub, and she was flying, crying out in ecstasy as her orgasm hit with shattering intensity.

While she was still limp and panting from her release Alistair rolled them over again, leaving her for only a moment while he reoriented his body to hers. His kiss was tender, and he settled his big body over hers with a gentleness that belied the need in his eyes. "I love you," he whispered against her lips.

"I love you too." She drew up her knees, inviting him to take her. "I want to do this with you forever."

"That's my intention." He laughed, his eyes gleaming with the love she knew was showing in her own expression. He gathered her hands in his and lifted them over her head, pinning them with one hand as he arched his hips and eased himself into her slick heat.

He made love to her slowly, both of them savoring each moment, lingering over every sensation and touch. Gradually their passion grew; gentle touches grew bolder, tenderness gave way to need. Her legs lifted and wrapped around his hips, urging him deeper with every panting thrust.

His lips never left hers, even their breath was shared. They moved as one, both of them completing what the other lacked. She felt her body tighten, arching up beneath him as her release began to build. His pleasure flooded her senses, and she knew he would be feeling the same, both of them feeding off the other in a perfect circle of give and take. He released her hands and pushed himself higher above her, dropping the last of his control as they once again raced towards their inevitable orgasms.

Keri's pulse raced, and her blood felt as though it was liquid light, singing and sparkling through her veins. Every nerve screamed with pleasure as he filled and stretched her, driving her to the edge of the abyss and then right over the edge into a whirlwind of blissful release.

Her body lifted and shuddered as she came undone beneath him and Alistair came hard, jet after jet of his semen leaving his body as he cried out her name again and again like a prayer.

Keri felt his warm breath fan over her neck and turned to kiss his cheek, laughing as she realized she barely had the energy to move. "I'm going to need to start drinking energy drinks just to keep up with you."

Alistair eased himself off of her and sprawled onto his back, tugging her up against his side as his breathing gradually returned to normal. "We'll be sure to bring some across next time we are in your world. I'll stock the house with them." He pressed a kiss to her hair and snuggled her in closer. "Anything my mate needs, we'll bring here."

She sighed in contentment and nodded. "I'll make a list for later. Right now, though, I think we better rest. Unless I am mistaken? I believe in a few hours we're supposed to be at your parents for dinner, and this time, I'm determined to be well rested and fully clothed."

He snorted with laughter, "They may not recognize you that way." He reached over to tug a blanket over them both and closed his eyes. "Welcome to my life, Beautiful."

EPILOGUE

Keri turned the final screw and set down her tools. "There, it's done." She stepped back to admire her handiwork, a proud smile on her face.

"It's beautiful." Alistair's arm snaked around her waist and tugged her into his side as they both looked at her creation.

The bed had taken her months to finish, but now it was done and assembled in her bedroom on Salt Spring. The entire frame was carved, sanded and polished by hand, the detailed work calling to mind a forest clearing. Just as she'd envisioned, the columns appeared as trees, the canopy made up of their interwoven branches.

They'd decided to split their time between the two planes, spending the spring and summer months on the island and then leaving for his home as the grey days of rain and dampness came to the west coast.

Many locals were snowbirds, taking off to warmer climes when winter came. No one had questioned it, and it had allowed her to keep part of her old life while embracing her new one.

She glanced up at Alistair, and her heart skipped over in her chest as it always did when she realized he was hers, forever. "Are you really alright with me bringing all my tools to your home when we settle there next week?" She asked.

"Of course, I am. By then the workspace will be ready for you, and I already know what your next project should be."

"I'm the artist, I'm supposed to decide on my own projects!" She punctuated her words by tapping her index finger against his broad chest.

"Don't you at least want to hear my idea?" He grinned at her, looking smugly handsome as he held her close.

Keri raised a brow, sensing he was up to something. "What's your idea then?"

"A crib." He murmured and leaned down to kiss her cheek as his hand smoothed down to span her stomach.

"But why would we need a— oh!" Keri's heart seemed too big for her chest suddenly, and her voice went low and very soft. "Really? You're sure?"

"Really." He grinned. "I wasn't expecting to have a family of my own for another century or more; you are magical, and I am the happiest daemon in all the planes. I have my mate, and soon, my child."

Keri beamed back, her eyes brimming with tears of joy as she lay her hands over his where they spanned her stomach. "It takes two to make this kind of magic."

"So it does." His lips found hers as he lifted her up and carried her over to their new bed. "Enchanted or not, I promise you'll not be able to leave this bed for at least a week."

Keri just laughed. She had no doubt the bed she had carved had a magic all its own; every part of it had been crafted with love, tears and thoughts of her beloved daemon. She'd made this bed for them.

He leaned down and kissed Keri tenderly. "I hope she has your beautiful hair."

Keri just grinned for a moment before replying, "He or she, I just hope they don't have your horns, at least not until *after* they are born!"

The End

ABOUT THE AUTHOR

Susan lives out on the Canadian west coast surrounded by open water, dear family, and good friends. She's jumped out of perfectly good airplanes on purpose and accidently swum with sharks on the Great Barrier Reef.

IF THE WORLD ENDS, SHE PLANS TO SURVIVE AS THE SPUNKY, COMEDIC SIDEKICK TO THE HEROES OF THE NEW WORLD, BECAUSE SHE'S TOO DAMNED SHORT AND OUT OF SHAPE TO MAKE IT ON HER OWN FOR LONG.

TO CONTACT HER ABOUT HER BOOKS OR TO ARRANGE END OF THE WORLD TEAM-UPS, YOU CAN EMAIL HER AT *susan@susanhayes.ca.*

For all titles by Susan Hayes, please visit her website:
susanhayes.ca

To keep up with her latest news, releases, and appearances you can join her newsletter:

http://eepurl.com/bd_GoH

SNEAK PEEK AT BOOK TWO

Release
Daemons and Angels book Two –

Raven Thorne dedicated her life to Cat's Cradle Sanctuary, her family's rescue center for big cats. When an unscrupulous resort developer sets his sights on her family's land, the gifted animal telepath finds her beloved sanctuary the target of sabotage.

Malyk is a daemon, an immortal being who has lost all joy in life. He is at a crossroads, unsure if he wants to continue his life or seek the release of oblivion. A chance encounter with one of Raven's errant charges gives him a momentary purpose: protect the beautiful mortal with a heart of gold and the courage of a tigress.

RELEASE

CHAPTER ONE

The lights were out again. Raven set down her book and navigated her way through the house to the kitchen by touch and memory. The wind howled against the windows as she tugged on a jacket and boots and grabbed a flashlight before heading out into the storm. She needed to start the generator and the check on the animals. This was the third power outage in a month, and there was no way it was an accident. First, something had tripped a breaker, and then the power line had somehow managed to get taken out by a falling tree branch on a windless day, and now this.

She tugged the collar of her jacket higher as a blast of chilled, rain-filled wind drained the warmth from her body. It was only early December, but this winter already promised to be colder than usual. "Maybe it'll snow, wouldn't that just be the icing on the cake," she muttered to herself as she played the flashlight over the pathway in an attempt to avoid the deeper puddles. The path needed to be repaved, but there was no money to do it. No money for anything more than the basics right now, not with donations at an all-time low and the bills piling up. Realizing her thoughts were as dark as the night, she scolded herself. "There's food in the fridge, a roof over the heads of yourself and your animals, and everyone is healthy, so stop complaining."

She was almost to the door when she heard it, a low, menacing growl out in the darkness. "Oh shit." She forced herself to take a deep breath and relax before walking the last few steps to the door and turning her back to it, feeling slightly better now she knew nothing could sneak up on her. She switched off the flashlight and waited while her eyes adjusted to the dark, trying to slow the hammering of her heart as the full weight of what had happened struck her. Someone had done more than just mess with the power this time. This time, they'd opened at least one of the enclosures. Things were getting out of hand.

Another growl sounded and this time, she could make out a shadow lurking in the darkness, moving slowly toward her. She reached out with her gift and sighed with relief as she recognized the thought patterns of one of her gentler charges. *Sometimes being a freak has advantages.*

"Paz my girl, c'mere." Raven crouched low and offered her hand to the animal prowling just beyond the limits of her vision. "You want to go home, don't you girl? You're not enjoying being out on your own." She kept her hand still, and a moment later she was rubbing the ears of a purring cougar. "Who let you out Topaz? Hmm?" She gazed into the cougar's amber eyes and touched the cat's thoughts briefly. Scents and shadowy shapes impressed themselves into Raven's mind. No face and only an impression of two men, one tall, one short and rounded. Raven sighed in frustration. "So much for getting answers the easy way."

Once she had the cougar calm, Raven removed the belt from her jeans and gently looped it around the cat's neck as a makeshift leash. "Let's get you back home girl, then I'll go turn on the lights and make sure no one else is loose." The last thing she needed was for some of her more aggressive charges to get off the property, which was very likely just what the saboteur had hoped for.

When her grandmother had started this place as a sanctuary for big cats, hers had been the only house for miles. There had been plenty of forest between the animals and any neighbours. But then Salt Spring Island had become a popular vacation spot, the population exploded, and these days there were neighbours all around the Cat's Cradle Sanctuary, and not all of them were keen about living beside a wild animal refuge. If one of her cats ever got out, her neighbours wouldn't stop until the entire sanctuary was shut down.

Raven checked out Topaz's habitat for tampering and then let the big cat enter. "Next time someone you don't know opens your gate, bite him for me."

Topaz just yawned in response and climbed to the top of her tree house.

Raven chuckled as she closed the gate. "Some guard cat you are."

The old generator started up without a fuss for once, and within minutes the lights were back on across the sanctuary. Fifteen acres of woods, fields, and shelters, all heavily fenced and gated to prevent the animals getting out. Raven could hear the chickens clucking in protest at the sudden flood of light, and she knew tomorrow she'd be seeing fewer eggs. One more inconvenience courtesy of Jerry Carter, resort developer and a major thorn in Raven's side.

As she checked the other enclosures, Raven's thoughts circled back to Carter and Evergreen Development Company. He'd seemed alright the first time he'd come to speak to her about selling, a bit slick maybe, his down-home accent and mannerisms a touch contrived, but for a salesman, he'd seemed fairly decent. As it turned out, each meeting he'd gotten more aggressive, and every time she'd refused to sell her family home he'd grown more determined to get his hands on it. At first, it had just been increasingly high offers and a barrage of phone and email contacts. But lately, he had started making veiled threats. Then some of her funding had dried up. Long term supporters had suddenly started finding other causes to donate to, and bills that had always been a little behind started coming in with angry red stamps of "overdue" and "immediate payment required."

She was nearly done her rounds when she found the second unlocked enclosure and an icy tendril of fear curled itself around her spine, Ares was loose. Out of the six big cats she had in her care, the black panther was the most dangerous. He'd only arrived a month ago, half starved to death and badly abused. They'd had to tranquilize him just to treat his injuries, and he had remained distant and distrustful ever since. Even with the talent, she had inherited from her mother's side she'd barely made any progress with him. The panther had refused to allow her to touch his mind, keeping up walls of pain and distrust she had not been able to breech.

Feeling vulnerable, Raven fought the urge to run as she headed back to the main barn to get the tranquilizer gun. Running would only attract his attention if the panther was still close enough to see her. She kept a steady pace as she tried to sense where Ares had gone, but she couldn't get more than a vague sense of direction and intent from Ares' mind. Unfortunately, a vague sense was more than enough. She broke into a sprint. He was heading for the tree line at the far side of the property, fast.

* * * *

Malyk was walking without a destination when he sensed the presence of a predator nearby and was overcome with curiosity. He'd never felt such ferocity before. He'd been out walking, something he had taken to doing each night after the island had grown dark and peaceful. He'd been too long away from humans and the constant shift and flow of their emotions, though welcome, could also be overwhelming.

He veered from the path and started making his way across country, ignoring the wind and rain as he picked up speed and ran toward the animal that gave off waves of aggression and fear as it prowled through the darkness. Since he'd arrived here a few weeks ago the island had proven to be as restful and idyllic as his half-brother, Alistair had promised, the perfect place for a daemon in need of a change. But it was also rather boring, and the angry creature he could sense promised to be a distraction.

It took him ten minutes to cover the distance between himself and his quarry, and he grinned the entire way. It had been too long since he'd last had a reason to run anywhere, too long since he'd had reason to do anything, really.

He found his quarry in a tree just inside a heavily built fence that stood fifteen feet high. It was a black panther, his coat marred with old scars and fresh ones, underweight, though Malyk did not sense the cat was currently hungry. He stopped at the fence and stared up at the cat, barely breathing hard. Despite knowing the creature couldn't truly understand his spoken words, Malyk found himself talking aloud. "What are you doing here? You're a long way from your kind, aren't you?"

The cat growled low in warning and Malyk could make out the angry lashing of his tail even in the darkness.

"You can see me, but I can see you too, so you might as well stop carrying on." He walked over to the fence, tensed his muscles briefly and then leapt over it, managing the feat with little effort and a hint of smugness as the cat stopped growling and stared at him, curious.

"And I know you can't do that, or you'd be on the other side of that fence already." Malyk laughed as he leaned against the bole of the tree the panther had climbed. "Since you can't leave, why don't you come down here?" He repeated the invitation mentally and watched as the big cat's eyes widened and then narrowed. He merely met the cat's gaze and let the animal see what he was: not human, not a threat, not prey.

* * * *

Raven's all-terrain vehicle rumbled through the night, anxiety causing her to grip the handlebars until her fingers turned white. *If Ares had managed to find a way over the fence, I'll lose the sanctuary. Please, oh please let him be safe and inside the fence.* She repeated the last phrase over and over as she drove, the rain half blinding her as it streamed through her hair and into her eyes. There had been no time to change into heavier rain gear, she'd just grabbed the tranquilizer gun, a snare pole and the keys to her ATV and started driving.

She was so distracted by worry that it wasn't until she stopped the ATV that she realized that Ares' mental presence was stronger and had grown more open and easier to read. There was no trace of fear or rage in the big cat's mind. Instead she could sense—contentment?

What's going on now? She grabbed the gun and flashlight and headed toward the cat on foot.

Her light bobbed and danced around the clearing as she tried to find Ares, finally landing on something that shouldn't have been there, a pair of long, denim-clad legs sticking out from behind a tree.

"Oh god, tell me you didn't eat someone, Ares!" she groaned and moved to see better, playing her light over what she feared was a dead body.

"Is that his name?" A faintly accented male voice asked as he lifted his hands to shield his eyes and the panther's from the blinding beam of Raven's flashlight.

Raven just stared. Seated at the base of the tree was the most attractive man she had ever seen. His blonde hair was long enough to hang over his shoulders, framing a face that would look more at home on the cover a magazine than lounging underneath a tree on her land. He had a strong jaw, lightly dusted with blonde stubble and his lips were turned up in a smile that made her quiver deep inside. He was just as soaking wet as she was, and sprawled across the handsome stranger's lap was Ares, one paw resting lightly on the man's impressively broad chest.

"I'd get up, but I just got him calm so it's probably best I stay put for now." The blonde gave Raven a grin and patted Ares' side. "My name is Mal. Does Ares belong to you?"

She blinked several times as if wondering if the strange apparition before her would vanish. When both man and cat stayed right where they were, she finally found her voice.

"Ares? He's under my care while he recovers." She raised a hand in greeting, her eyes still full of amazed confusion. "I'm Raven Thorne, and this is my land you're on."

She took a step closer and then froze when Ares opened an eye and growled at her. "How did you get him to do that? He won't let anyone else near him."

Mal laughed and shrugged his shoulders. "He was just in a great deal of pain. Whatever was done to him a while back, it left some internal damage that was not healing properly. It made him cranky."

Their gazes met, and Raven was surprised to realize his eyes were nearly the same shade of golden brown as the panther's. It was easy to make the comparison, as both pairs of golden brown orbs were focused on her. "He was pretty badly abused before we got him. This is a sanctuary; we've been trying to get him healthy again."

"He should be fine now." Mal gave the big cat another pat and then pushed him off as though he was a kitten and not more than one hundred pounds of muscle and claws. "Up you get, I think it's time you went home, Ares."

"He's fine now?" Raven glanced dubiously at the panther. "Later on, you can explain to me how that happened. For now, I have to figure out how to get him back home. I was expecting to have to drug him and drive him back." Raven frowned in thought as she glanced back toward where she'd parked the ATV. "I doubt he's going to just follow me home."

Malyk stood up, unfolding to his full height of well over six feet. He leaned down and dusted the worst of the mud and forest litter off of the oilskin jacket that fell past his knees. He made no attempt to hide his interest as his gaze wandered over her, making Raven feel like crossing her arms over her rain drenched chest. She knew he couldn't see much in the dark, not with her wearing a jacket and a heavy sweater that came down to mid-thigh, but somehow she felt exposed as he looked his fill and then gave her a slow smile.

"I could come with you? He'll follow me."

She felt his gaze still boring into her, and Raven nearly rejected his offer out of reflex. Then she remembered she still had to get Ares home. "I'd appreciate the help. The sooner he's safe and snug, the better. I need to get things settled, and I'm sure you are looking forward to getting home." She tilted her head slightly. "Wherever home may be. I've lived here my entire life, so I know you're not a local. Not with that accent."

He gestured back into the darkness, indicating the rise beyond her property. "I'm staying at my sister-in-law's house just up the hill, but no, I'm not from around here." Malyk snapped his fingers and Ares fell in beside him. "How long a walk is it back to your place?"

Raven tried to quell a surge of jealousy as Mal effortlessly brought Ares to heel. Normally she was the one who could quiet any cat, but Mal had done what she hadn't been able to, he'd gotten through to Ares.

"Too far for the weather tonight." She gestured for him to follow her and took the lead, grateful that he couldn't see her blush as she realized she'd have to drive them both back, which meant having the gorgeous blonde riding pillion. The thought of him having his arms around her made her breath catch in her throat, and her heart beat a little faster.

When they reached the ATV, she'd had him keep Ares calm as she started the motor, concerned the big cat would never stay put otherwise. With Mal's hand on him, though, the panther hadn't so much as twitched as the engine roared to life.

"You'll need to sit behind me and hang on," she told him, glancing to the rear of the ATV.

Mal raised a brow. "Interesting machine," he commented as he swung a leg easily over the seat and settled behind her, his strong arms wrapping around her waist and his thighs lying along hers.

She could feel his body heat seeping into the back, making her realize how cold she had gotten. Part of her wanted to lean into his warmth and enjoy the sensation of being held. It had been a long time since anyone had held her.

As if reading her thoughts, strong arms tugged her tight against him, and he spoke, his words a low rumble just by her ear, "You're cold."

"The sooner we get Ares tucked away, the sooner I can warm up." She moved her head to speak to him and then stopped when she realized his lips were still near her ear. If she looked back any farther... She let that thought go and wrestled her mind back to the task of driving them back across the sanctuary in the middle of a rainstorm.

The whole trip back Ares loped along beside them, never further away than she could see, even in the storm-torn darkness. Whatever Mal had done to Ares, it seemed to have made quite the impression.

She felt every bump and rut in the road on the drive back because every bounce pressed their bodies together and made her tingle from head to foot despite the fact she was soaking wet and chilled to the bone. As they arrived back at the main barn, she'd shut off the engine, but Malyk hadn't moved a muscle, his arms still wrapped around her waist, holding her firmly against him.

"You need to let go now." She twisted back in the seat and tapped his arm, reminding him he hadn't released her yet. "I have to get Ares back in his enclosure and see if I can't get the lights back on."

Malyk arched a blonde brow, clearly confused. "The lights *are* on, aren't they?" He gestured around them, water dripping off his sleeve as he did so.

"I'm using the backup generator. Whoever let Ares and Topaz out also messed with my power, again."

He was up and off the ATV in a heartbeat and scanned the area around them, looking for any threat. "Someone let Ares loose on purpose?"

Damn, he's tall. Her brain took a side trip to re-assess his looks now she could see him clearly. His hair was so blonde it was almost white, and the stubble on his jaw was only a shade or two darker. He had strong features, full lips, and cheekbones a model would kill for. What she could see of his body underneath the oilskin jacket confirmed what she already knew from the drive back, he was one well put together man, solid and strong.

Realizing she was staring and had yet to answer him, Raven groaned inwardly and snapped out of it. "It's not the first time they've messed with my equipment, but it's the first time they've let the animals out. I've tried to tighten security, but it's a big place." She swung her leg over the ATV seat and stood up.

"Do you think you can get Ares back home? It's just over here." She pointed to their left to where a chain link gate hung open.

Malyk nodded, snapped his fingers again and a minute later he was latching the gate as the big cat vanished into the darkness of his pen. "He's safe and secure."

"Thank you." She ran a hand through her soaking wet hair and winced as she realized what a wreck she was. "I really mean it. If you hadn't found Ares, he might have gotten over that fence and hurt himself, or someone else. That's got to be what they were hoping for."

"Who would do that and why?" Malyk's words had an edge to them now.

"Carter's men. They're the only enemies I've got." She paused, wondering how much to tell this stranger. For all, she knew he could be a spy for Evergreen Development.

Malyk seemed to sense her hesitation, and he paused for a moment before coming to some sort of decision. "You don't need to tell me Raven, I'm a stranger, I understand. But I'm also not going to leave you alone out here until we get the power back on, and I know you're safe back in your house. Whatever is going on here, you shouldn't be alone."

Raven blinked and stared at Mal. Had he just offered to protect her in a roundabout way? Things were getting bad, sure, but the last thing she needed was a guy with a hero complex coming to her rescue, or a spy, or—a really nice guy who happened to look like a living avatar of sin. She laughed at herself inwardly and threw caution to the wind. "Ares trusts you, so I will too. I could really use the help, thanks."

"Don't thank me yet, I haven't mentioned that I'm quite useless with tools and don't have the faintest idea how to fix your power problem," Malyk said with a grin, clearly pleased she had accepted his help.

"Let's start by checking the fuse box, maybe they just mess with it again. Anything more complicated and I'll just phone the power company in the morning and have them come out. At least we're going to get in out of the rain." She gestured for him to follow him as she headed to the main barn.

If you enjoyed Arousal

You might also enjoy:

The Summoned Series

Summoned and Sold
(The above book is permanently free)
Summoned and Stolen
Summoned and Bound

The Drift Series

Double Down
All In
Wild Card
Three of a Kind

Susan's books in the 3013 Series

3013: RENEGADE
3013: STOWAWAY
3013: TARGETED
3013: FATED
3013: SCARRED

www.ingramcontent.com/pod-product-compliance
Lightning Source LLC
Chambersburg PA
CBHW022214170626
46807CB00005B/2363